Kretz

From the Files of

Madison Finn

Read all the books about Madison Finn!

Coming Soon!

Don't miss Super Edition #1

From the Files of
Madison Finn

Super Edition #2:
Hit the Beach

By Laura Dower

HYPERION
New York

For all the fans

Text copyright © 2006 by Laura Dower

From the Files of Madison Finn is a registered trademark of Disney Enterprises, Inc.

Printed in the United States of America

First Edition
1 3 5 7 9 10 8 6 4 2

The main body of text of this book is set in 11.5-point Frutiger Roman.

ISBN 0-7868-3780-2

Visit www.hyperionbooksforchildren.com

Outside, the temperature in Far Hills topped ninety, but inside Madison Finn's bedroom, the air conditioning was on full blast. Mom had moved the TV into Madison's room for the night, and it cast a cool blue glow over the darkened room and everyone's faces. Everything about this night spelled the ultimate slumber-party setup: good snack food, great friends, and enough pillows for absolutely everyone. Phinnie lay across the top of the comforter gnawing on a rawhide bone, while Madison and her friends clustered together on the floor, gossiping, giggling, and munching away on a batch of Mom's cheddar popcorn.

"This is one of my all-time top ten favorites," Madison's BFF Lindsay Frost declared when the opening credits for the movie *Bring It On* came on screen.

"I still can't believe you've never seen this, Maddie," said Fiona Waters, another one of Madison's closest pals. "Like, have you been living in a cave?"

"No one ever takes me to the movies," Madison grumbled, acting as if she were truly upset.

"As if!" Madison's buddy Aimee Gillespie cried, tossing a small pillow directly at Madison's head.

Madison chuckled, because, as everyone in the room (including Phin) knew, she *had* just gone to the movies last week—with none other than Hart Jones, her übercrush for as long as she could remember. It wasn't a solo date, of course. Almost every one of their friends had accompanied Hart and Madison to the movies. But she and Hart *had* walked into the theater together, sat in seats next to each other, and shared a package of malted-milk balls. Their knees had certainly touched more than once.

Unfortunately for Madison, however, she wasn't going to be going to any more movies with Hart, not for a few weeks, anyway. She was headed for Florida to join her dad and her stepmother, Stephanie, who had rented a condominium for the month of August. They had enrolled Madison in an environmental learning program at a place called Camp Sunshine. Madison wasn't sure she liked the super-cheery name of the camp, but if it had to do with animals, she was willing to give it a chance.

She wasn't the only one leaving Far Hills for part of the summer. Fiona and her parents were headed for California to visit friends, and Lindsay was flying to London with her father. The only one of the four staying close to home was Aimee. An important dance performance was scheduled at the ballet studio in just a few weeks.

Knowing they'd be separated for a long time, the BFFs had decided to throw a good-bye slumber party at Madison's house. Mom helped out with the refreshments and the movie rentals (three videos, for an all-night marathon). In between laughter and gossip, the foursome tried to hold back the tears. Madison felt the mushiest about the prospect of not seeing her closest friends for nearly two weeks.

"I—just—can't—stop—thinking . . ." she sniffled at one sappy movie moment between two of the on-screen friends, "this reminds me of—when—we—"

"Maddie," Aimee groaned. "Get ahold of yourself."

Fiona passed a box of tissues to Madison while Lindsay gave Madison an over-the-shoulder squeeze to let her know that she would be missing everyone, too. Then Aimee joined in. It was hard not to cry.

"Is everyone okay in here?" Mom asked from the doorway. She'd passed by and heard the sniffling.

"Yup," Madison said, still hugging Aimee and Lindsay at the same time.

"We're just missing each other already," Fiona added.

Mom grinned. "So these are all good tears, huh?"

"Yeah," Lindsay sniffled. "Good-*bye* tears."

"Rowwrrooooooooooo!" Phinnie howled, as if on cue.

Then everyone had to laugh.

"Well," Mom said, turning away from the doorway, "I'll leave you girls to your Kleenex. Turn off the TV before you go to sleep. That is, *if* you go to sleep."

"Yeah," Madison giggled. She took a deep breath so that there would be no more tears. "Thanks again for everything, Mom."

"No problem, honey bear," Mom said, walking out of the room.

The movie wasn't over, but the four girls weren't as interested in watching its ending as they were in finding creative ways to stay awake all night. Aimee suggested that they log on to Madison's computer to see if there were anything interesting they could do online.

"Let's check bigfishbowl.com and find out what will happen on our summer vacations," Madison said.

"Great idea!" Fiona chimed in. "Maybe it'll predict my future with Egg, too."

Aimee pinched her nose, and Madison laughed.

They plugged in Madison's laptop and headed for bigfishbowl.com, making a beeline for the special fortune-telling section of the site: ASK THE BLOWFISH.

4

Madison asked the fish her question first.

Will Camp Sunshine be fun?

Before Madison could click the ANSWER button, Lindsay let out a loud laugh.

"I still can't believe you're going somewhere called Camp *Sunshine*," Lindsay chuckled. "I'm sorry, Maddie, but that sounds so dorky."

"Hey, sunshine is good," Fiona said. "I like sunshine. California is sunny. . . ."

"Nah, it's dorky," Madison moaned. "And naturally, that makes me Queen Dork, right?"

"Only sometimes," Aimee joked.

The four friends looked up at the laptop screen expectantly as the Blowfish finally revealed the answer to Madison's question.

Will be yours for a long time.

"Huh?" Madison asked the screen. "What is *that* supposed to mean?"

"I think it should have said, *will be dorky for a long time*," Aimee cracked.

"Ha-ha," Madison sneered, poking Aimee in the shoulder.

"Someone else, ask a question, please!" Fiona said.

"Okay, okay, I've got one," Lindsay spoke up. "Will I meet someone cool in London?"

Madison began to type Lindsay's question in.

"Someone cool?" Aimee asked. "Or someone *cute*?"

Lindsay began to giggle. "Both."

The Blowfish swam around in its onscreen bowl before releasing its answer in a giant bubble.

Put out your hand and reach for happiness.

The four girls stared blankly back at the answer on the screen.

"That sounds nice," Lindsay said. "But what does it mean?"

"Let me try a question," Aimee said. She exhaled deeply and typed her message on the keyboard. *Will I get to perform the solo I want at the dance show?*

Aimee pressed the Blowfish, but no answer appeared. Instead, Madison's laptop hissed, the screen flashed blue, and the power zapped off—just like that.

"Wow. That's not a good sign," Aimee sighed. She smiled. "I killed the Blowfish."

Everyone laughed—except Madison.

"My laptop keeps doing this," Madison groaned. She tried pressing the power button, but the machine wouldn't turn back on. "Let me see—if—I—can—fix it. . . ."

Lindsay threw herself down across a pile of pillows. "You know, we should convince our parents to take a vacation together sometime," she said.

Aimee nodded. "That would be the *best*." She glanced over at Madison. After all, they'd spent a winter break together skiing—and it had been a special experience for both of them.

Phinnie nudged Lindsay's bare feet with his cold

nose, and she let out a little yelp. Aimee grabbed Phin's paws and pretended to dance with him, twirling him around until he lost his balance and rolled on to his back. Phin cooed as Fiona scratched his bare pink belly. He was in doggy heaven with all the attention.

Meanwhile, Madison continued to poke at the keys on her laptop, hoping for some kind of result. It wouldn't turn on.

"Maddie, what's going on with Hart?" Aimee asked Madison all of a sudden. "Put down the laptop and fess up."

"Are you keeping secrets from us?" Fiona said. "Chet said he saw you guys walking the dogs in the park yesterday."

"What's the real deal?" Lindsay asked.

"There is no real deal," Madison replied. "You guys know everything."

"Did Hart say he was going to miss you this summer?" Aimee teased.

"No. We agreed to e-mail while I'm in Florida," Madison said, "but that doesn't mean anything."

"Sure it doesn't," Aimee cracked.

"Quit it, Aim." Madison shot her BFF a stern look. "Watch out, or I'll start talking about Ben Buckley."

Aimee picked up one of the pillows from the bed and hurled it right at Madison's head. "You wouldn't dare!" Aimee shrieked.

Madison threw the pillow back at Aimee. Then

Lindsay and Fiona got in on the action, and they picked up their own pillows. Little goose-down feathers from inside a couple of the pillows flew into the air and back down on to the carpet. Fiona thumped Madison across the back. It was a full-blown pillow war.

"Gotcha," Aimee cried out, aiming her pillow at a new target.

Lindsay sideswiped Fiona, who fell to the floor, narrowly missing Phin. He quickly darted out of the way and hid underneath the bed.

The foursome broke into a chorus of laughter that had Madison snorting (in a funny way) and wiping tears of joy from her eyes. In no time, they collapsed on to each other, legs and arms intertwined on the blankets.

"Thanks for having a slumber party," Fiona said.

They clustered together for a group hug as Aimee grabbed her digital camera to take a photograph. Aimee held the camera out, and everyone squeezed together to get into the frame.

"BFFs forever!" Madison said.

"Um . . . you know that means Best Friends Forever Forever, right?" Lindsay inquired.

"Really?" Madison said.

"Aw, who cares, Lindsay?" Aimee cried. She socked Lindsay in the shoulder with her free hand. "You are such a stickler for grammar. Geesh. No wonder our English teachers love you."

"Yeah," Madison smiled at Lindsay. "But I love you, too."

" 'Forever forever' is better anyway," Fiona added, sticking her tongue out at Aimee.

Aimee snapped a picture of Fiona's funny face. Then she took at least ten other digital photos—each with different facial expressions, such as smiles, poked-out-tongues, frowns, kissy faces, and other funny poses. After the extended photo session, the girls collapsed backward again on to the pillows. It was getting late, and they were getting tired.

But none of the girls let herself get *too* relaxed. It was still too early to go to sleep. They had a whole night of adventure ahead of them.

Madison turned the radio on low so they could listen to tunes while they gave each other pedicures. She pulled out a plastic container that held different buffers, bottles of polish, and other tools. Fiona polished Aimee's toes, and Madison polished Lindsay's. They decided to paint all of their toes the same coral-pink color. After they'd switched partners and everyone's toes were painted, they turned the lights off completely and stretched out on their sleeping bags in the center of Madison's room, with toes in the air so the polish could dry. The girls took up all the floor space, while Phin slept by himself up on Madison's bed.

Long after the toenails had dried and Phin had fallen asleep (and started his deep, doggy snoring), the girls shared secrets in the half-darkness. The full moon outside Madison's room was like a permanent night-light, and they could see the silhouettes of one another's faces as they talked.

"I wonder what it will be like to see all of my old friends in Los Gatos," Fiona mused. "I mean, I don't remember ever feeling as close to them as I feel to you guys right now."

"You'll have a great time," Madison whispered. "I promise."

"I wish I was seeing old friends," Lindsay said. "But no. I'll be stuck with my dad in London the entire time."

"We really should keep in touch when we're away," Aimee said.

"I'll send a postcard from California," Fiona said.

"I will, too," Lindsay said.

"No, we should keep in touch every day," Madison said. "Like we do now. We should e-mail every day. We can pick a chat room and a time to talk."

"But we can't," Fiona said. "Can we? I mean, when it's six here it'll be three in California and some other time in the middle of the morning in England."

"Oh," Madison said. "Well, we could try."

"We could try," Lindsay seconded her.

Aimee was about to say something, but yawned instead. "I'm so tired all of a sudden," she said. She rested her head on the pillow inside her sleeping bag. Fiona curled up in her own sleeping bag under one of her mother's warm quilts. She needed a blanket, because the air conditioner in Madison's room was still turned to the high setting.

The radio played an old Alanis Morissette tune. At first, Lindsay and Fiona quietly hummed along. No one was really talking anymore. Madison felt her own eyelids droop. Then, no one was humming, either.

"I don't want to say good night," Madison whispered in the dark.

No one said anything back. Madison glanced around the room and saw that no one's eyes were open anymore. Everyone had dozed off for real, even though it was only midnight.

Madison leaned over, clicked off the radio, and scrunched down inside her fluffy sleeping bag. She felt something hard inside the bottom but realized it was just one of Phin's squeaky toys.

"Good night, everyone," she whispered aloud.

Then, just like that, she headed off to dreamland with everyone else.

And although this was the first stop on the long road to each of their summer vacations, Madison knew that her *real* journey had scarcely begun.

Chapter 2

The cursor blinked on the screen of Madison's laptop, and she breathed a huge sigh of relief.

It was finally working again.

She'd spent the morning with Aimee, Fiona, and Lindsay—getting dressed, tidying up the bedroom, and then invading the kitchen where Mom had made plates of hot scrambled eggs and peanut-buttered whole-wheat toast for everyone (except Fiona, who took her toast with jam only, no peanut butter, *ever*). The morning had flown by, and soon the girls had been standing on the front porch, eyes wet, going through yet another round of "Good-bye, I love you, I miss you, I can't believe I won't see you" tears. It was all pretty exhausting, Madison told herself when the last good-bye had finally been said and she stood all alone in her living room again. Of course, she wasn't exactly *alone*. Mom was there— somewhere in the house—working on the outline for her latest project with Budge Films. And Phin was there, too, sniffing at his now-empty dish of kibble. He'd had a few eggs and peanut-butter-and-toast crusts, but was still hungry for more.

Madison didn't let her alone-time get her down. Instead, she took it as a perfect opportunity to get her laptop working again. Was the battery dying? Was her hard drive sick? Had she contracted some kind of shutdown virus—maybe from hours spent trolling around the Internet? She needed to find out.

Phin turned out to be good company as Madison performed the umpteenth computer checkup. He nuzzled her ankles, making noises only occasionally, when he wanted a quick scratch behind the ears or on the snout.

In the end, the laptop started up, without prob- lems this time, which meant that it had no clearly identifiable ailment. This fact only made Madison more frustrated. How could she be sure the thing wouldn't black out again?

"Everyone's gone already?" Mom cried as she dashed into the kitchen to refresh her mug of green tea.

Madison shot her a funny look. "An hour ago, Mom. Where have you been?"

"Oh," Mom said, her eyes looking a bit glazed. "Sorry, honey bear. I've been preoccupied with some work this morning."

Mom took her cup and sat on a pile of cushions atop a sofa.

"So?" Mom asked expectantly. "What are you working on now? Shouldn't you be packing?"

"I have to deal with the laptop first. It crashed again," Madison explained.

"Again?" Mom cried. "Aw, Maddie, you should just leave it at home. Do you really have to bring it to Florida? I could have one of the tech guys from work check it out."

"No way, Mom. I need my files with me at all times," Madison said, aghast at her mom's suggestion. "Especially since I'm going away."

"Of course," Mom said, trying to sound soothing. She changed the subject and sipped her tea. "Maddie, your dad is right. This camp seems made for you. It's just the spot for a budding environmentalist and scientist. You know, I saw nesting turtles once, and it was quite exciting."

"Yeah, but you saw turtles in the Galapagos Islands," Madison said. "I'm just going to Florida. That isn't nearly as cool."

Mom grinned. "Turtles are turtles, Maddie," she said. "Nature is beautiful *everywhere*. Remember that."

"I know," Madison said with a shrug.

14

"So," Mom hinted gently, "when were you think-ing about packing that suitcase? Hmmm?"

Madison took the hint. As usual, she had saved all of her clothes-packing for the last minute. At Mom's reminder, she bounded upstairs to her bed-room to stuff a suitcase (or two). The flight was scheduled from LaGuardia Airport in New York to West Palm Beach in Florida for later that very evening—at 5:20 P.M.

Madison started to pack, but instantly became overwhelmed. She fell on to her bed and stared up at the ceiling.

"Oh . . . what should I bring, Phin?" Madison asked.

If dogs had really been able to talk—i.e., speak English—Phin probably would have woofed, "Bring me!" Unfortunately, Madison had to leave the dog in Far Hills. And he had no fashion tips.

Madison decided she didn't have time to con-template her wardrobe anymore. She was in a race against the clock. Madison plowed through the closet, plucking one or two sundresses off their hangers. Shorts! She grabbed some denim shorts, then black, olive green, navy, and a new pair of orange ones, and folded them together, placing them in a side section of the suitcase. A handful of white, pink, blue, and yellow T-shirts completed the pile. Then she packed a white, eyeleted top she'd gotten from Boop-Dee-Doop's online catalog but never

15

worn, a blue baby-doll top with spaghetti straps, a pair of faded jeans, a long pair of linen pants (perfect for dinner out with Dad and Stephanie), and a dozen or so other tops and bottoms, including a pair of shocking-pink capri pants that she loved to wear—even if she probably would have to endure being compared to a flamingo at some point during the trip.

Madison wondered what the other kids at Camp Sunshine would be like. Since there was no stringent prerequisite for admission to the camp except for a basic love of science, Madison guessed that the group of kids she met would be just like her—only from different parts of the U.S. Or would they? The more she thought about leaving the comfort of Far Hills for the sticky, slimy heat of Florida in summer, the more Madison began to doubt.

For starters, how could she make it without her BFFs so far from home? Could she last two whole weeks without her beloved Phinnie? Way back in the spring, when Dad had suggested the camp stay—to coincide with a short business trip and a vacation that he and Stephanie were taking in Florida—Madison had been thrilled to sign up. She had relished the idea of beach walks and long talks with Dad under the palm trees. But now—now that camp was really and truly here, she wasn't so sure. The only thing she was certain to get in Florida was sunburned.

Madison climbed on top of her stuffed suitcase

and pushed down hard so she could zip up the side. It was a delightful sound, that final *zzzzzzzip*, and she was happier than happy finally to be packed. After shoving a pair of flip-flops and a pair of sneakers into one of the outside pockets, Madison gave herself a thumbs-up. The hardest part was done.

Madison had only two hours before her departure.

She turned once again to her laptop, frantically checking to make absolutely sure that she had all the e-mail addresses and other information she needed to keep updating her files during the two-week trip. Then she logged on to bigfishbowl.com. To Madison's surprise, her e-mailbox was no longer empty.

FROM	SUBJECT
✉ JeffFinn	C U SOON
✉ BalletGrl	I luv u more than ballet
✉ GoGramma	My new e-mail address

The first, from Dad, was about the trip, of course. Madison hit REPLY.

```
From: MadFinn
To: JeffFinn
Subject: Re: C U Soon
Date: Sat 7 Aug 12:45 PM
```
Dad, you are sooooo funny. Quit making me NERVOUS writing to me right before I get on the plane!

17

:>) Yes, I remembered to pack everything the camp requested that we bring. (I have the checklist in case we need it.) I have one fat suitcase and I'm carrying my sleeping bag as a carry-on along with my orange bag and laptop. BTW: Thanks for reminding me about the security at the airport. I'll wear rubber-soled sandals so I don't set off the machines. Duh I almost forgot when I did that last time and U got so freaked out when they pulled me aside and opened all my bags. As if I was some kind of security risk, right? Guess it's better 2 B safe but still . . .

OK I am so rambling. FYI I will be in West Palm Bch around 8 PM I guess or sooner. You better check. Will Stephanie come 2 the airport? Can we go to dinner @ that cool place u told me about?

See you at the baggage claim. Don't be LATE :>)

xox

Maddie

Madison clicked SEND. Then she looked at the next e-mail, from Aimee. She laughed to herself when she reread the subject line.

```
From: BalletGrl
To: MadFinn, Wetwinz, LuvNstuff
Subject: I luv u more than ballet
Date: Sat 7 Aug 12:49 PM
```

Seriously!!! I do!!! OMG that was THE BEST sleepover EVER, Maddie. Right? U know it's totally not me to be the mushiest of the BFF group but I am feeling sososososo sad AND 100% mushy right now knowing I won't see ANY of u for like 2 wks. OMGOMGOMG! I'm crying right now I swear. My brothers think I am the hugest LAME-O. But u understand, doncha? I so wish I wasn't the only one sticking around here in Far Hills. *sigh* E ME from the airplane! LOL J/K.

LYLAS,

Aim

There was an e-mail from Gramma Helen, too, but Madison had only just clicked on it when she heard the doorbell downstairs. She stopped to listen.

"Hello," she heard Mom say; her voice was friendly, but faraway. Madison couldn't hear anything else she was saying. She figured the person at the door was someone from Budge Films, or maybe just the mailman or the delivery guy.

"Maddie?"

Madison pricked up her ears. Mom was calling her. Maybe Aimee was there? That would be just like Aimee to write a sappy e-mail and then dash over to Madison's house in person so she could embarrassingly take it all back. Chuckling to herself, Madison leaped off her bed and went into the hall.

"Did you call me, Mom?" Madison asked from the top of the stairs.

"I sure did," Mom said, coming into view. "You have a visitor."

Madison grinned and bounded down the stairs. "I know who it is," Madison said with a smile. "Aimee, you just couldn't stay away, could you?"

All at once, Madison stopped. It wasn't Aimee.

It was Hart. *Hart*.

"Sorry to just come over like this, Finnster," Hart said. "I tried e-mailing you, but it kept coming back to me. I think my e-mail account is messed up. Sorry."

"Um . . . that's okay."

Madison didn't know what else to say—she was that surprised. Her mind was spinning like a hamster's wheel. All she could think about was how cute Hart looked in his skater T-shirt and long shorts. His hair was growing out a little bit. He had one of those dreamy tans. She hadn't really noticed it until just then.

"Anyway," Hart went on, "I forgot that I wasn't going to see you for a few weeks. I didn't want you to leave without saying good-bye."

"Oh," Madison bowed her head down. "That was so nice."

Hart reached for Madison's hand. She gave it to him and he squeezed it. But then Mom walked back into the room and they both let go—right away.

"So, Hart, are you staying? Should I make a snack?" Mom asked. It was a little after two-thirty in the afternoon.

Madison hoped he would say, "I'm totally here for a snack, and in fact, I've decided that I'm following Madison to Florida, because I can't bear to be without her. . . ." As usual, she was letting her imagination run wild. But Hart wasn't really saying anything like that.

Hart shrugged. "I can't really stay that long," he mumbled. "I just wanted to . . . um . . . you know . . . um . . ."

"What?" Mom crossed her arms.

Madison took a breath. *Why wasn't Mom going back into the kitchen and leaving her and Hart alone?* Just her presence was making Hart super nervous.

"Yeah. So . . ." Hart said, turning to Madison.

"So . . ." Madison said.

"So?" Mom said. She still didn't get it. Madison wanted to wail—loudly.

"Okay. Well. I better go," Hart said. "I just wanted to say, like I said, I wanted to stay, I mean, *say* . . ."

Mom looked at Hart. Then, as if hit by a lightning bolt, she finally—*finally*—got it. She glanced at Madison, who made a face that said, *Please*, please *leave right now, Mom, so I can be alone with the boy I have had a crush on for as long as I can remember.*

"Oh, my goodness, I just remembered I left something on the stove," Mom said quickly.

Good lie, Mom.

No, it was a great lie. Mom disappeared back into the kitchen.

"I'm so sorry," Madison stammered. She smiled at Hart. "Um . . . you were saying . . ."

Hart reached for her hand again right away.

"What I was saying was . . ." Hart looked around nervously. "Is your mom gone for real or is she gonna jump out from behind the couch?"

"She's gone," Madison reassured him with a laugh.

Hart appeared convinced. "What I wanted to say was that . . . well . . . I want to remember you, you know, just like this, right here," Hart said.

Madison felt her stomach flip-flop.

"You want to remember me standing here in my hallway?" Madison joked nervously.

Now his fingers were both squeezing and pulling. Was Hart pulling her toward him?

Madison froze.

Hart leaned forward. What was she supposed to do now? Madison was way too freaked out to register what was going on. The word *kiss* popped into her head, but she chased it away. This couldn't be it, could it? Their first kiss? The moment she'd dreamed about a hundred times? *Now?*

"Rowwrororooooooooooo!" Phin barked. He leaped out of nowhere, right up on to Hart's leg, nearly knocking him to the floor.

A very superstitious Madison had to take that as a sign.

Not now.

As Hart straightened up again, he clutched Phin in his arms. "Anyway," he muttered, "you will E me, won't you, Maddie?"

"Of course. I'll E you every day," Madison gushed. She desperately wanted to throw herself forward and plant a big, fat kiss on Hart's lips. That would have been a real movie move. But wanting to do something and actually doing it were two completely different things. This wasn't a kiss moment, not even in slow motion. This was freeze-frame—all the way.

After another silence, the moment was completely gone.

Hart walked over to the front door. Madison

followed like a puppy, and the real puppy, Phin, followed, too.

"Thanks," Hart said for no reason. "Um . . ."

"No. Thanks to *you* for coming over. It was a total surprise. Wow." Madison tried to fill in all of the quiet between them.

"I never expected . . ." she said. "Well, you know. It was so nice. You are so nice."

"You, too. But you know that. Look, have a good time at camp," Hart said at the doorway.

"And have a good time being a lifeguard at the pool," Madison said.

Phin dashed over and began licking Hart's leg. Madison tried to grab the pug, but his curlicue tail slipped through her fingers.

Hart grinned a wide grin. "I really will miss you, Finnster," Hart said. "Really. And I'll even miss Phin, too. Right, buddy?"

Phin panted extra hard, as if he understood.

Madison smiled at them both. "Good-bye, then."

"Yeah . . . bye . . . for real, now," he said, walking down the porch steps. He gave Madison a little half-salute before stuffing his hands into his cargo-shorts pockets and heading back down the street in the direction of Fiona's and her twin brother Chet's. Madison figured he must be going there to play Wiffle ball or video games or just to chill and talk about boy stuff, whatever that might be. She turned around and closed the front door. Her skin was all prickly—but in a good way.

"I can't believe that just happened!" Madison gasped out loud.

Mom raced out of the kitchen wiping her hands on a towel. "What happened?" she asked with a little wink.

"Mom!" Madison said, looking embarrassed.

"I hate to put pressure on you, honey bear, but we need to get going in the next twenty minutes or so," Mom said. "We may hit traffic on the way to the airport. You can't miss this plane."

Madison glanced at the clock. It was now after three. She still needed to finish the packing and the laptop prep and *go*. The race was on.

Lucky for Madison, the Hart Jones butterflies still fluttering in her stomach had the power to lift her into the air, up the stairs, and right into her bedroom. That was what it felt like, anyway.

As Madison pulled together the final items for her two-week trip, she tried to imagine how Camp Sunshine could possibly make her feel any sunnier than she felt right just then.

Chapter 3

Since she was still under thirteen and flying solo, Madison needed to be escorted on to the plane earlier than the other passengers. She hated the way everyone waiting at the gate stared as the flight attendants helped her aboard. It made her feel like a little kid.

But it was very cool to board a plane that was completely empty. The air was cool, fresh. The seats were empty. She walked a short distance to the sixth row in coach. She had the window seat, as she had requested. If she was lucky, Madison would be able to catch a glimpse of the New York City skyline as the plane took off.

Slowly, after Madison had sat down, placed her

carry-on bag in the overhead compartment, and made herself (and her laptop) comfortable, a steady stream of passengers entered the plane. Everyone stared again as they passed by Madison's seat. Madison tried her best to ignore them. After a few minutes, an older man with a boarding pass in one hand and a hardcover novel in the other stopped at Madison's row of seats.

"Excuse me, but are you in the right seat?" he croaked.

Madison grabbed her boarding pass and held it up.

"Oh, yeah," the man sighed. "I got the aisle again. I told that travel agent I wanted the dang window. Golly."

"I can switch if you want," Madison said softly, trying to be nice.

The man's face lit up. "Why, aren't you a dear, sweet thing?" he said, clearing his throat at the same time. Then he waved her off and sat down in the aisle seat. "Not to worry. I'll make do with the aisle seat."

Madison giggled nervously, hoping that the man wouldn't say anything else to her on the long flight.

But of course, that was not to be. The man, whose name Madison later discovered was Walton (or Wally, for short), was some kind of scientist. He studied wildlife. Or was it sea life? Madison wasn't exactly sure. He was on his way to Florida to meet his wife and the rest of his family. They lived down there for part of the year. The only other thing Madison wound up knowing for sure about him was that Wally loved to talk. She listened for almost two hours to Wally's war stories: about trips he'd taken to places like Antarctica and about really, *really* big fish.

It was *not* what Madison had expected. By the time the plane neared Florida, her ears were tired. But she listened some more anyway. She didn't want to be rude.

"Listen to me prattle on," Wally said as the pilot announced the initial descent to the West Palm Beach airport.

"I like it," Madison said. "I mean, I liked your stories. I want to be a writer one day. I think. Well, a writer and a vet. And maybe a biologist. I'm not sure which."

"Those are big dreams," Wally said. "Good for you."

"Thanks."

"So, tell me something else."

"Tell you something *else*?" Madison crinkled her brow and shook her head, not sure what he wanted to know. "Like what?" she asked. She felt the plane swoop down a few thousand feet more. They were almost there.

"You know, you remind me of my wife, Myrtle,"

Wally said. "And my great-granddaughter, Myrtle Junior, of course."

"Myrtle *Junior*?" Madison asked with a smile. "That's different."

"How old are you, anyway. Sixteen? Seventeen?"

Madison burst into giggles. "I'm twelve, sir," she said.

"Ah, yes." He waved Madison off. "These days it's all the same to me," he muttered, almost to himself. "When you get to be my age, everyone under sixty seems like a baby."

"How old are you?" Madison asked casually, not wanting to offend him.

Wally looked at her and smiled. "Eighty-one," he said proudly.

"You remind me a little of my Gramma Helen," Madison said, "only older."

"So, I guess that means we're practically related," Wally said.

Madison laughed again. Wally was like a lucky charm. He'd changed her mood, made her forget any airplane jitters she had had, and—most importantly— helped her get over the sadness of leaving Far Hills, her BFFs, and Hart.

The flight attendant came by and asked everyone to buckle up and prepare for landing.

As the 747 pulled up to the gate and attached itself to the proper Jetway bridge, the plane began to buzz with the sounds of people shifting in their seats, unbuckling seat belts, and moving bags. Cell phones appeared like magic. Everyone seemed to have someone to call.

Wally shook his head and leaned over to Madison.

"Don't ever let yourself get caught up in all this craziness. . . ." He pointed to the people standing around with phones at their ears.

Madison nodded. "Oh, yeah?"

Wally squinted at her and lowered his voice some more.

"If you just stop and listen, you can change the world, you know," he said, and Madison knew he meant it. "You're an excellent listener. I can tell. You notice things. Things that other people don't. I can tell."

"So, I can change the world, huh?" Madison asked.

"You bet. All it takes is one. That's what I always told my Myrtles," Wally said. "You just have to understand that we're sharing the world—all of us— the people, the animals, the water. It's for sharing, not taking."

Madison thought Wally sounded a little like one of the Zen philosophers Aimee's mom liked to listen to on her meditation and yoga tapes. She was glad she'd met him.

Wally collected his things and headed for the exit along with everyone else. He gave Madison a little salute before fading into the flow of people; his gesture reminded Madison of Hart's salute back in Far Hills. Madison's chest tightened. Did good-byes ever get easy?

The flight attendant came over and made sure Madison was okay leaving the plane. Of course, she was. After all, she wasn't a little kid. The walk to the gate seemed to take an eternity. And then Madison strolled out under the bright fluorescent lights of the airport.

Madison made her way to the baggage-claim area, accompanied by a nice lady who worked for the airline. As Madison came into view, Dad and Stephanie waved madly. "Here! Over here, Maddie!" Dad shouted.

Madison broke into a grin and raced over to her father. The three of them squeezed together in a hug and then went to get Madison's luggage. As they walked over to the baggage carousel, Madison searched the crowd for Wally. But he was nowhere to be found.

They got Madison's suitcase and headed outside to the parking lot. The air was like mashed potatoes—sticky and thick. No breezes blew.

"Welcome to Florida in the summer," Dad announced. "Not my first choice, but it's a lot cooler by the water where we're staying. We're in this area where the Indian River meets the ocean. No matter how hot it gets, there's always some kind of breeze. You'll love it."

"So, Madison, did you have a pleasant trip?" Stephanie asked.

"Yes," Madison said. "I sat next to this really old guy. He talked a lot. But he was cool. Actually, he talked a lot about animals."

"Did you tell him you were going to Camp Sunshine?" Stephanie asked.

"Why would she tell him about Camp Sunshine?" Dad interjected.

"Because," Stephanie said. "She was making conversation."

"Anyway . . ." Madison said in a cheery voice. She leaned toward the front seat a little bit.

"Hey," Dad cautioned, "shouldn't you have your seat belt on?"

Madison leaned back and buckled up. "Sorry," she mumbled.

"No," Dad said. "I didn't mean to snap. You hungry?"

Stephanie turned around. "You e-mailed your dad about going to that cool restaurant we were telling you about," she said, "so we made a reservation."

"The place is called Seashores," Dad said. "You'll love it."

"Way cool," Madison said, gazing out of the car window. She stared at the scenery as they drove away from the airport.

Madison saw rows of lush palm trees and

32

bougainvillea. She saw brightly colored stucco homes and office buildings with enormous shutters. She knew that hurricane season was there, although Dad assured her that the forecasters had predicted no major storms for the month of August—at least not yet.

After a short drive, they drove up a long ramp on to an enormous bridge. There was water everywhere Madison looked. Off in the horizon she saw the ocean, foamy waves breaking at the shore. All along the edge of the water, set back from the beach, Madison spotted apartment buildings and mansions. She could see everything from way up there on the bridge. Dad slowed the car down and pointed to a small, overgrown island in the center of the river under the bridge.

"That's called Pelican Isle," Dad said. "I just found out about it. I think Camp Sunshine takes a boat trip near there."

"Really?" Madison asked, nose pressed to the window.

"The more I hear about this camp," Stephanie said, "the more impressed I am. In fact, your father and I were just taking a look at the camp brochure before we picked you up at the airport."

"You were?"

"I want this to be a special summer trip for you," Dad said, reaching back for Madison's hand.

Madison took his hand and smiled.

"Thanks, Dad," she said. "I know it will be."

She let go of Dad's hand and hunkered down again in the backseat. She stared out the window and counted the other small islands dotting the river. If only it hadn't been so terribly hot there in Florida, Madison thought. She was grateful that Dad and Stephanie had the air-conditioning on high just then. It would take her time to get used to the temperature—*lots of* time.

Madison wished her laptop had been working better, or, rather, working at all. She'd tried it once on the airplane (when Wally had gotten up to stretch his legs), but it had just sizzled and gone off before she had had a chance to log on. If it had been working, Madison could have e-mailed everyone right now: Aimee, Fiona, Lindsay, and even Bigwheels, her long-distance keypal. If Madison's pals couldn't be there with her in the car, or at camp, then she craved the next best thing: virtual contact.

Dad and Stephanie drove north. After a while, they finally pulled the car into the jam-packed parking lot of the restaurant. Madison saw a huge sign in the shape of a swordfish. It said SEASHORES. A parking valet dressed in a flowered shirt and shorts took Dad's car as the three of them headed inside.

Dad had told Madison that not only was the food

at Seashores delicious, but also the restaurant was known as one of the best waterfront dining locations on the coast. The front of the restaurant was a designated waiting room, since the lines for dinner were always longer than long. Madison dipped her fingers into a tank full of skate fish and stroked the smooth tops of a few while she waited with Dad and Stephanie for their table. Then she gazed at an enormous lobster aquarium off on one side of the waiting area. Lobsters climbed all over each other in a kind of tank dance.

As Madison stared at the tank for at least five minutes, she imagined Aimee back home, dancing. She thought about Fiona, too, arriving at the Los Angeles airport armed with a soccer ball, her lucky stuffed bear, and her annoying twin brother, Chet. And she imagined Lindsay making her way through the London airport with her nose stuck in a book, as usual.

Were her BFFs thinking of Madison, too, at that exact moment?

She hoped so.

Although they were all so far away, Madison felt her BFFs close to her, like warm breath. They were as close as the green-black lobsters, the wide ocean, and the promise of the unexpected at Camp Sunshine.

Somehow, knowing they were out there—anywhere—made *all* the difference.

WELCOME TO

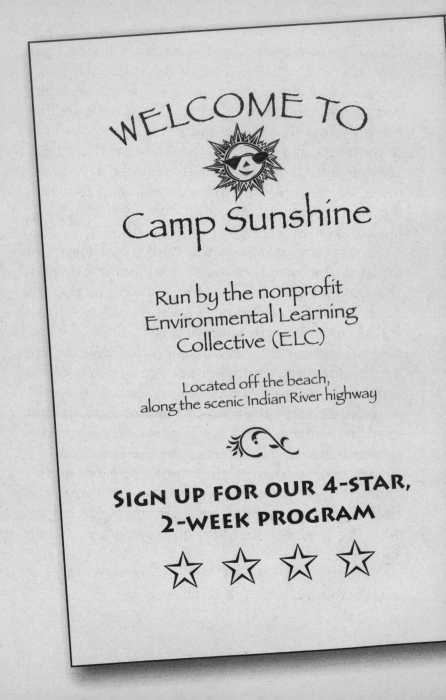

Camp Sunshine

Run by the nonprofit Environmental Learning Collective (ELC)

Located off the beach,
along the scenic Indian River highway

SIGN UP FOR OUR 4-STAR, 2-WEEK PROGRAM

ALL ECOSYSTEMS GO!

Spend two weeks with other kids exploring the many ecosystems and creatures found along Florida's Indian River and Atlantic coastline. Camp enrollment includes classroom and outdoor and environmental games, puzzles, and team-building projects. Ages 11 to 14. Registration required.

- *Birding 101:* Ride a real pontoon; head for Pelican Isle as you learn about all of Florida's wild birds.
- *Team Seagrass:* Study puffers, pipefish, shrimp, flounders, and other wildlife inside seagrass beds.
- *Full-Moon Turtle Walk:* Study loggerhead turtle nests along the shore; then observe hatchlings up close (night trip).
- *Manatee Watch, Interactive Games, and more:* As you study and play on our 45-acre campus, you may get wet and dirty. Please see a learning center supervisor for details on appropriate attire for all registrants.

Help Us Find the Explorer in YOU!

Chapter 4

The morning after arriving in Florida, Madison awoke to bright sunlight pouring into her room at Dad's rental apartment. The walls were painted salmon pink, so when the early light hit them, everything turned a sort-of-pink hue, too, including Madison's skin tone.

Mmmm.

Madison sat up in bed and rubbed her eyes. Without a pug to nuzzle her toes in the morning, Madison felt a little lost, but she could hear the ocean, and that made up a little bit for missing Phin. Easy, pounding surf could be very calming and exciting all at the same time. The morning put a fresh face on everything. She was there! Camp was there!

Rereading the Camp Sunshine flyer in the car the night before had made everything sound amazing all over again. Madison had nearly forgotten about the planned bird-watching and manatee-watching and about spying on really big turtles. With so much to do, she'd have no time to stress out about her friends or to miss Hart, would she? And the previous night's dinner at the seaside restaurant had sealed the deal. Just touching those skates in their aquarium had turned Madison from Far Hills computer girl to Florida nature girl *like that.*

However, when Mom had called to check in, Madison had expressed doubts about being in Florida. That was when Mom had reminded Madison about one of Gramma Helen's favorite aphorisms: "Positive-think—and your ship won't sink."

Gramma Helen's words of wisdom made Madison laugh. They were a lot like the words of wisdom Wally had dished out on the plane. Madison shut her eyes and tried to remember—word for word—what it was that Wally had said. She wanted to write a few of Wally's wise words down for posterity. With her laptop on her lap, Madison smoothed out the coverlet on the bed, pressed the power key, and waited for something to happen.

When she saw the laptop light go on, Madison breathed a sigh of relief, although she wondered if the computer were simply giving some kind of great big show before it conked out again.

Would it be working when she needed it most? Or not?

Over the next two weeks, Madison would almost certainly have to pester Dad to let her use *his* computer when hers wasn't working properly. And she would have to do it often—just so that she could check to see when and how many times her friends had e-mailed her from their different corners of the planet.

But for now . . . she had a file to write.

Summer Vacation (So Far)

Just one more day of free time before camp starts.

My gloom and doom prediction: RAIN for the first day of Camp Sunshine.

Oh! Am I just being bitter right now because a little, teeny piece of me misses Far Hills--and my crush--so much??? Aaaaaaaah!

Vacations are always this major conflict for me. I love trying new things (sometimes). But I love the warm, fuzzy, familiar things WAY better. It's too bad there's no one super special to share it with me.

Rude Awakening: Someone once said absence makes the heart grow fonder. But I wonder: does it make the Hart (as in Jones) grow fonder, too?

Okay, I'm being ridiculous. I haven't even been here a full day and already I'm making a mega-drama about Hart and me being separated. I have to stop. All that drama queen stuff belongs to my mortal enemy, Poison Ivy, right? Not moi. LOL.

Dad's apartment is pretty cool, I have to admit. He and Stephanie rented it from some music producer guy (he owed Dad a favor, apparently). There is the best stereo system and huge plasma TV and it's crazy big. Well, it's bigger than Dad's place in Far Hills anyway. It has a lap pool outside and this huge patio.

Now that I am here, I'm nervous about camp. I'm hoping (fingers and toes crossed, natch) that the other kids will be cooler than cool. I mean, new friends in Florida won't be half as cool as old friends back home, but

Madison paused and stared at what she'd written. She heard a knock, very soft, at her bedroom door.

"Maddie, are you up yet?"

Stephanie gently pushed the door open and saw Madison sitting there under the covers, laptop on her knees.

"I woke up and decided to check my e-mail," Madison said with a wide yawn. "Before my laptop crashes again."

"I should have known," Stephanie said with a

smile. She pulled the drapes open in Madison's room, and even more light flooded inside.

Madison shielded her eyes. She snapped her laptop shut and jumped out of bed. There was a crystal-clear view of the pool and patio from her window.

"Your dad had to head out for an emergency business meeting this morning," Stephanie said.

"He's not here?" Madison asked.

Stephanie shook her head. "It's just us girls, at least this morning. So I was thinking that maybe we could have a girls' day out. We could take a long walk on the beach, maybe collect a few seashells?"

"A walk sounds good," Madison said cheerily. She needed to do something besides sit inside and brood about Hart.

"I can show you the little beach town and we can stop for lunch at Lemon Drop," Stephanie went on. "It's this old rock-and-roll-diner-style restaurant downtown."

"Sounds fab," Madison nodded in agreement. "You always have good ideas."

Stephanie left Madison to get dressed. They agreed to head out in a half hour—just enough time for Madison to grab cereal and for Stephanie to make herself another enormous mug of green tea.

It was only ten in the morning and the beach was already steamy-hot. The sun pounded down on the back of Madison's neck. She could practically feel the sunburn happening. They walked for about half a mile along the beach, kicking around in the foamy tide and scanning the beach for colored shells and beach glass. Madison spotted a large piece of blue glass that was shaped like a heart. She shoved it deep into the pocket of her shorts.

I can give this piece to Hart, she thought. It was his favorite color—and the perfect shape, to boot.

Stephanie found a large conch shell. There was a chip on one side but it was, for the most part, intact. Madison held it up to her ear.

"I remember when I was a little girl, Mom told me that you could hear the ocean inside one of these," Madison mused.

Stephanie laughed. "But you can!" she insisted. "Can't you?"

Madison laughed, too.

There were not many other people on the beach. It was a little too hot, even for the locals. There was a slight breeze along the water, however, that made the temperature more bearable. Madison figured it was just a matter of getting used to things. After a short time, she was actually beginning to *like* the heat. It helped that Stephanie had lent her a large straw hat that kept the bright sun off Madison's face.

Stephanie already had a flawless tan. She worked out at the gym every day, and her browned skin accentuated the look of her curves and muscles. Madison thought Stephanie looked a little bit like a model, especially in her white bikini and flashy green sarong. Sometimes Madison wondered how Dad could have married someone who was so different—who looked so different—from Mom.

Madison looked down at her own bathing-suit top. It was polka-dotted with a gold loop tied at the center. She'd found it on the sale rack at the mall just the week before, when Mom and she had gone shopping together for her camp stay. The bottoms were more like shorts than bikini pants. Madison liked the way it fit.

"Look!" Stephanie cried, pointing ahead of them on the sand.

A clear, corked bottle had washed up on the shore. Madison raced over to it and looked inside.

"Oh, wow!" Madison cried, breathlessly. "There's something inside!" She fingered the cork, but it wouldn't come out. Stephanie came over to help. She was able to wedge the cork out with a loud *pop*.

The two exchanged excited glances.

"What do you think it is?" Stephanie asked Madison.

"A note! A real note in a bottle!" Madison cried.

Stephanie stuck her fingers inside and grabbed the note with a long fingernail. Madison was so excited about the discovery that she started jumping up and down.

"What does it say? What does it say?" Madison asked.

Stephanie unraveled the note. It smelled a lot like fishy seawater, although it was as dry as a bone. The ink was not smudged, but the handwriting was very sloppy.

To someone else:
   I am at the beach w/ my family and thought it would be fun 2 write in a bottle just like this. So here I am in the Bahamas and where r u? Send me a note back in a bottle 2, ok? I will be waiting.

Bye,
Jonas

"I'll be waiting?" Madison furrowed her brow. "That doesn't make any sense. Does it?"

Stephanie laughed. "Looks like someone was having a bit of fun," she said. "I'll bet Jonas is on vacation with his parents—and bored."

"But he actually thinks someone will write back to him in another bottle?" Madison asked.

"Apparently so," Stephanie replied. "Silly boy."

Madison and Stephanie looked at each other and burst into laughter.

Although Madison was tempted to shove the note back into the bottle and toss the bottle back into the sea, she didn't. Instead, she clutched it in one hand. She decided to keep it. She wanted to write about it in one of her files. Maybe the bottle was a good omen.

The sand felt gritty under Madison's toes as she and Stephanie walked further down the beach. By now, they had collected not only a conch shell, the note in the bottle, numerous shards of beach glass, and smaller shells, but they'd also found thirty cents, an old silver barrette, and a lot of seaweed. They were careful to sidestep the little patches of tar on the beach.

An hour later, Stephanie suggested that they go on to Lemon Drop for some food and drink. Madison was parched. No sooner had they sat down than she drank an entire glass of water in one gulp.

The waitress took their orders and then brought two extra-large glasses of lemonade.

"I am so glad you're here, Maddie," Stephanie said, "and I know your dad is glad, too."

"Is that why he's at work? On a *Sunday*?" Madison said. She hadn't meant to sound snappish, but that was the way it came out.

Stephanie frowned. "It couldn't be helped, Maddie," Stephanie explained. "He's in some nego- tiations with a client this week. You know that."

"I know," Madison said. She was used to both of her parents working all the time, overtime. But then again, Stephanie was there. That counted for a lot.

"You haven't told me anything about what's

going on back at home," Stephanie said. "I mean, you covered all the basics at dinner last night, but I want to know the real, undercover scoop. For example, how is that boy you like? Isn't his name Hart?"

"Yes. Hart," Madison said softly. "You remembered."

"Of course," Stephanie said with a nod. "How is he?"

"Same," Madison said, giving hardly any answer at all. She always felt self-conscious discussing boyfriends and crushes with grown-ups.

"Maybe you'll meet another boy at camp this summer," Stephanie said.

"Maybe," Madison said blankly. Inside her head, she was screaming, *But how? There is no other boy for me!*

The waitress brought their chicken-salad sandwiches with pickles and chips on the side.

"So, do you miss your friends yet?" Stephanie asked. She was hitting all the sensitive subjects.

Madison nodded. "I do."

"When I was your age, I used to go away to camp during the summers in Texas," Stephanie said. "My camp was called Home on the Range. Each summer I looked forward to camp for one big reason—and it wasn't the horses."

Madison giggled. "Was it because of a boy?" she asked.

"You betcha," Stephanie said, putting on her Texas twang. "I spent three whole summers pining after this one cute boy named Jed. He was one of the best riders at camp."

"Oh, so he was a *cowboy*?" Madison joked.

"Ha-ha," Stephanie laughed, acknowledging the wordplay. "All I remember is that he was my dream-boat, that's for sure."

"Did you ever hold hands, or . . . even . . . um . . . kiss?"

Stephanie raised her eyebrows. "Who wants to know?" Then she smiled. "Sure. We smooched. Behind a barn. Just a few times, I swear."

"I'm *so* telling Dad!" Madison squealed.

"What about you?" Stephanie asked.

"What about me *what*?"

"Did you and Hart ever?"

"What?"

Stephanie stared hard at Madison. "Kiss?" she asked.

Madison felt herself blush like red, red roses.

"Not exactly," Madison admitted. "We came close, though. I think."

"I see."

"We sort of held hands and his face got really close to mine, but . . . the fact is that Mom says I'm way too young to date and kiss."

"Oh," Stephanie said.

"What does that mean?"

"I think maybe she's right," Stephanie said. "What do *you* think?"

"I don't know," Madison said. "Well, I know I'm still really young. It's just hard, because it feels like everyone around me is doing even *more* than kissing. I mean, shouldn't I be doing more by now, too?"

"No, sweetie. Not at all," Stephanie said. "Maddie, you're still so young. There's plenty of time for that. Believe me."

"But . . . what if I really want to kiss Hart?" Madison asked. She lowered her head. "You know, I already had a first kiss—but it wasn't with Hart. It was with this boy Mark. I kissed him at Gramma Helen's house. Just once. It was during this fireworks show."

"Well," Stephanie said. "That's big news."

"But I never told Dad."

"Thanks for telling me," Stephanie said.

"You have to keep it a secret," Madison said. "Promise?"

Stephanie pretended to zip her lips shut. "So where's Mark now?"

Madison shrugged. "I was so lame. I never e-mailed him. He never e-mailed me, either, but still . . . it was just . . . I don't know what happened. I came home after the vacation, and then I started crushing on Hart right away again."

"Well, sometimes life is one big curveball,"

Stephanie said quietly. "But you really shouldn't rush anything, Maddie. Take your time when it comes to all that love stuff. There are a lot of things you can explore and enjoy that have absolutely nothing to do with boys."

"I know," Madison sighed. "Gosh, I can't believe I just told you all that. I told you about Mark!"

"Don't worry," Stephanie said as she bit into a pickle.

After lunch, Stephanie and Madison headed back to the apartment, grabbed a handful of miniature chocolate-chip cookies, and then went for a long swim in the pool. The water was like a bath, it was so warm. Madison swam a few laps each using the backstroke, crawl, and sidestroke. She also tried to do handstands, even though she kept flipping over backward before she could poke her feet straight out of the water.

Whether under the water or above it, Madison's thoughts kept drifting to Hart. She pictured him sitting on the lifeguard tower at the Far Hills pool. He knew how to do a backflip off the diving board. In fact, he was one of the best swimmers she'd ever met.

After their swim, Madison and Stephanie sat on the patio for at least an hour without talking, just enjoying the clear, hot skies. Madison had left her laptop inside so she could read her tattered copy of the latest Princess Diaries book instead. She flipped through a copy of *Seventeen* that Stephanie had picked up at the drugstore. Sitting there in the tropical air, amid the patio chairs, bottled water, and magazines, Madison felt as though she were living the lush life. She was no longer the girl who liked computers and crushed on boys who called her Finnster.

She was like someone in an MTV video. LOL.

Chapter 5

Dad came home late from his important work meeting, but he came bearing dinner: Chinese food from Lucky Chang, a too-cool restaurant near the offices where he'd been meeting all day. Madison had read about Lucky Chang—it was the kind of place where famous people went to eat and drink.

Stephanie set the patio table outside, and they ate by the pool. The clouds turned a deep orange-pink, and the sun dropped down in the sky. Everything was perfect—almost.

Madison had a pang inside.

Dad noticed that something was wrong. He guessed aloud that maybe Madison was upset because he hadn't been able to spend the day with them, but Madison assured him that she wasn't upset.

"I'm just homesick," Madison admitted. "Well, more like friend-sick."

"Hmmm," Dad said thoughtfully when Madison told him what was bugging her. "Maybe we can fix that feeling."

"How can we do that?" Madison asked.

"Try your laptop."

"Huh?"

Madison told Dad that Insta-Messages and chat rooms were too hard to manage with all the time differences.

Dad shook his head. "No, no, I was thinking of something else. What about a blog?" he suggested.

Madison slapped her forehead. "Of course! A blog!" she exclaimed. "Why didn't I think of that? Dad, you're a genius."

"I know," Dad said, not very modestly.

Stephanie just rolled her eyes. "It *is* an excellent idea, Jeff. If Madison keeps a blog—and all her friends do the same—everyone can stay updated on all the little stuff. After all, that's what matters."

"Right," Madison said, grinning from ear to ear.

"It will be a little bit like a one-sided conversation," Dad went on, "but I think it might help ease some of your separation angst. I mean, you are here for two weeks. That's a long time for you."

"Too long!" Madison agreed. "I mean, I'm happy to be here, but, I mean . . ."

"I know what you mean," Dad said reassuringly.

Since Madison's laptop had been acting up, Dad helped Madison set up a blog page on his office computer. She immediately forwarded an e-mail with all the automatic sign-up information for the blog to her friends. Individual pages would be created through the bigfishbowl Web site. The whole process was way easier than Madison could have imagined.

Before Madison could enter her simple profile, the screen prompted her to select a password. This would keep her blog page secure.

A single word popped into her mind.

It wasn't *Hart* (although the thought of him did cross her mind).

It wasn't *friend*, either.

The word Madison had thought of was the one that honored the person who had just that very moment made her feel truly hopeful about the coming weeks: *Dad.* Although he had been gone earlier that day, Dad had still come through (as usual) for Madison.

She quickly typed up her brief profile and added her first official blog entry before drifting off to sleep.

Name: MadFinn
Country: United States
State: Florida (right now n e way)

Gender: Female
Favorite color: Orange
Interests: Computers, reading, playing flute, animals, esp. cute pugs!!!
Expertise: Worrying (& missing my BFFs!)

08-08
Ta Da! I can't believe it but I really have my own blog page. You always told me I should do this, Aim. Dad showed me how & it's so E-Z. So now we ALL have to do it and then it will be like we're having a slumber party long distance from California to NY to Florida and all the way to England. I didn't do much today except get a suntan and walk on the beach BUT it's way cool because I collected all these shells. I decided that while I'm here I want to make you each something. I'm thinking about just the right thing. My camp starts tomorrow. I'm clueless about that. HELP! What r u doing wherever u r? Write yr own page sooner than soon. Miss you more than n e thing.

It was a short entry, but it said all the right stuff. Madison hit SAVE BLOG and shut off the laptop.

She fell asleep hoping that by the following afternoon her BFFs would add their own blogs to the mix. She also couldn't wait to tell Bigwheels about the blog page, since Bigwheels had had her page up for months.

Soon Madison Francesca Finn would be back in touch not only with her friends, but with her old self again.

* * *

The next morning, Stephanie was in the kitchen making coffee. Madison could smell it brewing. She glanced at the alarm clock on her nightstand, one of the old-fashioned wind-up kind. She'd forgotten to set it. But that didn't matter. She was up.

The first day of Camp Sunshine was here, but all Madison could think about doing was checking her brand-new blog again.

When she opened the page, Madison saw that it had already been read twice. She guessed the identity of the reader, which was confirmed when she saw a posted message from Aimee.

Madison clicked on a posted link to Aimee's new blog page.

Name: BalletGrl
Country: United States
State: NY
Gender: Female
Favorite color: Purple or pink or anything pretty
Interests: Ballet and dance
Expertise: ???

08-08 (late)
This is the best idea on the planet, Maddie. You deserve a big round of applause (<><><>)--that was hands clapping--I just made that up! :>) So Far Hills is Xactly the same as when you three left. Except that it was supposed to

56

thunderstorm today, which is cool since it's been too hot l8ly. I have not much to report fm here xcept that everyone is spending most of their time (as far as I can tell) FRYING by the town pool. Major hottie alert: that kid who just moved in down the street from you, Maddie; he looks cuter than ever. OMG. But I don't have time for boys NEmore except Ben Buckley. LOL. Seriously, I have already had one intense day of dancing since u left. And I GOT THE SOLO!!! Madame said I showed great progress esp. on pointe. Isn't that good?! FYI: when I was coming out of rehearsal yesterday I saw none other than Ms. Poison Ivy the Terrible on the sidewalk and she was alone (i.e., just parents and no drones) and she actually said HELLO to me. I almost passed out but figured she might think I had a real heart attack or something LOL. OK. So here's more big news 4 you: my dad is expanding his cyber bookstore. I guess that's not really a big deal 2 anyone but me & my family, but I wanted to share. Oh, and I also wanted to say that Lindsay prob. won't get her blog started right away. She called last nite b/c her plane was canceled to London. She and her dad didn't even leave until midnight or something crazy. She says HELLO tho. Where's Fiona? GTG now. More rehearsal. I swear I swear I swear I will write in this every day if I can. Peace out and LYLAS.

Madison laughed out loud at her BFF's first blog page. Then she clicked around to get to the next one. Not surprisingly, it was from Fiona.

Name: Wetwinz
Country: United States
State: (CA) (NY) (Outer Space--ha!)
Gender: F
Favorite color: red or orange
Interests: soccer, computers, friendship
Expertise: penalty kicks :>)

08-08
I MISS YOU ALL! Maddie, thanx for doing this.
Thank yr dad too, 'k? Yes, I am in California. Los
Angeles, to be exact. Or, Land of La, as my mom likes to
call it. I thought we might go to northern CA to see our
old house, but we came here first / instead. It is really nice
temps here for the summer. I wish I could come back
more. In two nights we go back to Los Gatos to stay
with my Uncle Ron and see our old neighbors and all
that. For now, we're just hanging by Disneyland. I've
never been here. Maddie, aren't u near Disney World in
FLA? It's like we're in the same place--only different, you
know? Well, enough of that. Chet is being as
annoying as ever. Sometimes I wish he'd just evaporate.
All he does is play video games. The only thing that's
sort of funny is that he was telling me he misses Egg and
Drew and Dan and the other guys a lot. So maybe the
guys aren't so different from us BFFs, right? BTW I also
talked to Lindsay right b4 we left. She told me (FYI) that
she dropped by the animal clinic and saw Dan there.
They talked a lot she said but she couldn't tell if he

liked her or not. Maddie--she pretended to fool him by saying she was at the clinic 2 see u when really (of course) it was 2 see DAN. WTG, Lindsay! Over to you guys. I will write more and more when we get to Northern CA.

C U! :>P

Lindsay had been to the animal clinic to catch up with Dan? Madison could hardly believe it. Just a few weeks before, she'd been nervous about the idea of even seeing him, let alone going someplace specifically to see him.

Madison chuckled at the thought of Dan and Lindsay chatting by the animal cages. Maybe he could get Lindsay to help him mop the floor or feed the birds. Lindsay would probably do anything to get his attention at that point.

Madison wanted to post another note on her blog right away, but she couldn't. She needed to shower and get set for the first day at Camp Sunshine. Dad was planning to drive her there in exactly one hour.

After a warm shower, Madison debated for twenty minutes about which outfit she would wear. She finally settled on the too-pink capri pants and a little white T-shirt that said HAPPY CAMPER that she'd borrowed from Fiona earlier in the summer. It seemed like the right (and fun) thing to wear to a first day of camp, although she tried on just about every T-shirt in her suitcase before making a final decision. Madison had never been a big part of the whole camp scene, so this was a learning curve for her. She wanted to proceed with caution.

Stephanie and Dad seemed to be even more eager than Madison for the start of camp. Madison offered to trade places with Dad, and everyone had a good laugh.

When they pulled up in front of the Environmental Learning Collective building, Madison saw the oversize flag waving out in front with a picture of an enormous sun with a smiley face and long rays.

"Welcome to Camp Sunshine," Madison muttered under her breath from the backseat of the car.

Stephanie turned around. "Don't sound so excited," she joked.

"I'm just nervous," Madison said.

"What are you afraid of?" Dad piped up. "A few fish? Manatees? Sand?"

"Dad," Madison groaned. "Quit kidding around. You know."

"You'll be the star," Dad insisted. "Everyone will want to be friends with you, because you are just cooler than anyone else."

"Great, Dad. Your saying that is like the kiss of death."

Stephanie snickered. "Try not to be so encouraging, Jeff," she teased.

Madison grabbed her backpack and popped out

of the car first. Stephanie followed, and Dad parked the car.

Once inside, Madison found herself face to face with a wall of turtle shells and petrified fish. She looked up to see stuffed birds, mangrove branches, and other objects hanging from the ceiling. It was as if nature had just exploded by the front door—but in a good way. Off on both sides, other kids waited for the camp directors to come out and lead them into the auditorium.

Stephanie and Dad hung around for a few minutes, long enough to know that they didn't really need to be there. Madison would be able to handle the rest on her own.

She gave both Dad and Stephanie quick pecks on the cheek, so as not to appear too clingy. Madison wanted to make the right first impression. Hanging on to Dad's arm pleading, "Don't go," wouldn't have gone over very well in any crowd, but especially this one.

"I know you'll love it," Dad said for the tenth time since they'd left home that morning.

Madison nodded and literally nudged him toward the door. Stephanie followed. And then Madison was alone—or, at least, on her own.

This is exactly why I have never ever gone to camp before, Madison thought.

She knew two weeks wasn't a very long time, but right now Madison imagined it as an eternity.

"Are you here for Camp Sunshine?" a woman with a mop of gray hair and gold-framed glasses asked Madison.

Madison nodded. "Yes, yes. Am I in the right place?" she asked nervously.

"Absolutely. Stay put. We'll be 'round soon to get you."

Madison stayed put. She browsed through some books on a bookshelf with titles like *Aquatic Journey* and *The Life of the Tortoise*. On one wall was a huge map of the area. Trees, bodies of water, and buildings were clearly marked. Madison noticed one small lake (was it big enough to be classified as a lake or was it more like a pond?) called Madison Bog. She smiled broadly at that discovery. She was afraid to be here, and yet she'd been here all along—at least in one form or another. *Even if it was a bog.*

"Nice shirt," a young boy said. Madison glanced down at her tee and the words *Happy Camper*.

The boy pushed back a thick strand of his blond hair and grinned. "Seriously, I like it. It's cool to watch turtles lay eggs. Doncha think?"

Madison nodded. "Yeah," she said. "That's just what I was thinking."

"So, who are you? I mean, what's your name?"

"Madison. But most of my friends call me Maddie."

"I like Madison better," the boy said. "It sounds smarter. By the way, I'm Will, and that's short for

62

William. Most of my friends call me crazy."

"Nice to meet you, Crazy," Madison said with a smile.

"I'm in eighth grade. How about you?"

"Seventh," Madison replied. Then she asked, "Are you from Florida?"

"Nah, I'm a New Yorker," Will said.

"I live in New York, too."

"Really? I live on the Upper West Side. Where do you live?"

Madison gave him a vacant stare. She realized he was talking about New York *City* when of course she was talking about Far Hills.

"Oh, no, I don't live right in the city. I mean, I live in . . ."

"The *burbs*, right?" Will said with disdain.

Madison couldn't tell whether Will was being serious or whether he was teasing. And if he were teasing, what gave him the nerve? She looked away, embarrassed.

But Will didn't notice. He was already facing in the opposite direction, talking to another camper.

Madison turned around herself and nearly knocked over another girl.

"Hi, I'm from Cleveland," the girl said, practically thrusting her hand into Madison's for a shake. "Ann's my name. Science is my game. Ha-ha. Well, you know. I'm one of those science geeks who can't get enough science."

She had feather earrings on, she was about Madison's height, and she talked with a bit of an accent that Madison couldn't quite identify. Madison tried to be as friendly as possible.

"Hey, Ann," she said sweetly.

"How great is this?" Ann said in a much louder voice. "I mean, meeting you like—whammo! You remind me so much of my best girlfriend back in Ohio. I can tell that we will totally become best friends during camp. Totally."

"Yeah?" Madison pasted on a smile. She appreciated Ann's enthusiasm, but she wasn't convinced about Ann's prediction. After all, the title of "best friend" was reserved for the elite few—and those few were not in the room.

But Madison didn't want to seem rude or to blow Ann off, so she started talking some more, about school and science. Ann loved to talk. She wouldn't stop babbling about herself or asking obscure questions. She did have some finer points, however. Like her jersey. It was a bright orange color—Madison's favorite color in the whole world—and Madison figured that that fact had to be one positive sign.

Or was it just a *sneaky* omen?

Chapter 6

Leonard, the camp director, finally showed up, a few minutes late. To get everyone's attention, he clapped his hands, then grinned a wide, crocodile smile. Madison wasn't sure what to make of him.

"Welcome to another summer together!" Leonard cried. "We're so happy to have old campers and new campers alike."

The kids cheered. Madison glanced around. *Old campers?* Almost everyone Madison could see from where she was had on camp T-shirts from the year before. It was like some kind of club meeting—only Madison hadn't really been invited, at least, not yet. They were all paired off already, too, which didn't seem altogether fair.

The guy she'd just met, Will, was standing with

another boy. Ann had cornered some other girl across the room.

There was that pang again.

Aimee? Fiona? Lindsay? Hart? Where are you?

Madison wisely scoped out the room, searching for new campers like herself. She saw a boy wearing a visor, sitting quietly in a corner of the room. He raised his eyebrows every time the director said something. Madison tried to make eye contact, and he grinned. She moved over to him.

"Hey," Madison said, trying to be friendly. "I'm Madison."

"Yo, hey. I'm Anthony, but I go by 'Tony' some-times," Anthony said. "Or Teeny. My friends call me Teeny. It's all good."

"Sure," Madison said. "Um . . . do you have a partner?"

Tony did not have a partner—so he agreed to be hers. Madison breathed a sigh of relief. She was off to a better start now, or at least, she hoped she was.

Having a partner for the camp tour reminded Madison of having a buddy for fire drills in elementary school. Madison remembered how back then she and Ivy had always been fire-drill buddies. They'd held hands—tight—on the way down the stairs to the outside of the building, and no matter how many times they had tripped on the steps, neither of them had ever let go.

It was funny how things had changed so

dramatically since then. Since elementary school, it seemed as if they were letting go all the time.

Leonard led the group of campers around. Madison counted at least twenty-five kids. Everyone was whispering, pointing, and, except for her, embracing old friends.

Teeny and another boy started talking, but Madison kept moving, following Leonard. Maybe she didn't need a buddy.

She listened as Leonard started to point out the different buildings on the property.

First, he took the entire group over to an old atrium covered with mangroves. Inside, Madison saw clusters of white, purple, and pink orchids, among other plants. There were a few wild birds flying around, too.

Around the corner from the atrium was a more modern, wooden-shingled building. Leonard showed all the campers into a room filled with exhibits on camouflage, animal tracks, and underwater life.

Adjacent to the exhibit room was the ELC Aquatic Center (at least, that was what the carved wooden sign said). Inside were individual tanks of fish and turtles and way too many snakes. Leonard told everyone to have a look around.

On one side of the room, Madison saw an enormous, open tank with another skate like the ones at the restaurant, as well as crabs, smaller fish, and sea grass. She moved toward it.

"Cool stuff, right? Did you see the turtle wall?"

Madison turned around. Will was standing there.

"Turtle wall?" Madison said. "No. Where?"

Will pointed to the corner of the room opposite the place where they stood. Up on the wall was a row of turtle shells and little plaques with text underneath describing the different turtle breeds. Madison read the plaques quickly. She had a lot to learn in the next two weeks.

"Okay, everyone," Leonard announced. "That's a quick tour for you. Now, follow me back to the main auditorium so we can split up into smaller groups."

"What does Leonard mean about splitting up into groups?" Madison asked Will.

Will ran his fingers through his hair. Madison stared, then quickly looked away when she realized she was staring.

"Well," Will explained. "It's like this. We do some things as a large group. I think there are, like, twenty or thirty people or something. We barbecue or play games together. Or have marsh walks. That kind of stuff. But for the studying—and the hatchling night, which I think is the best part of all—we work in groups of five or six."

"Five or six?" Madison asked. "How do the camp leaders split us up?"

Will shrugged. "Leonard pulls names out of a hat. I don't know. He sees who you hang with. Look,

68

I have no clue. I know he tries to mix it up so people meet new people."

"Wow," Madison said. "So we spend the two weeks with mainly five or six campers?"

"Pretty much," Will replied. "Plus, the camp leaders, of course. They swap around, so we work with everyone at some point. Some leaders are turtle experts. Other ones are fish experts. Some are just, like, nature police to make sure we don't destroy the grounds. Last year some kid got mad for no reason and ripped out all these plants. He got sent home."

"Gee, you know a lot about this place," Madison said.

"Well, yeah," Will said. "My grandfather—his name was Will, too—was one of the people who started it up. He was a conservationist. That's what Mom calls him. . . ."

"Someone who conserves nature and wildlife," Madison said simply.

"You're really smart, aren't you?" Will asked.

Once again, Madison couldn't quite tell if Will was being serious or if he was joking around. But she chuckled a little, deciding on the latter. She also found herself staring at him just a little bit again. She wasn't sure why. Something about him seemed nice, almost familiar.

"It must have been cool having a grandfather who made a place like this," Madison said.

"Yeah," Will said. "I've hung out here during summers and winter breaks from school ever since I was a kid."

Madison and Will followed the other kids out the door. Leonard lead the way. Someone grabbed Madison's elbow. It was Ann.

"Don't forget me-e-e-e-e!" Ann said.

Madison smiled politely, even though Ann had pinched her skin as she grabbed her. Madison tried to wriggle free without making a big deal out of it.

All at once, Teeny appeared. He poked Madison in the side.

"Yo, where did you go?" Teeny asked.

"I'm sorry," she said, trying hard to look contrite. "I thought you were talking to someone. . . ."

"Yeah, for, like, two seconds I talked to someone, and then you were gone. I thought we were going to be partners."

Madison glanced at Will and then Ann and then back at Teeny.

"Hey, Teeny," Madison said. "Do you know Will and Ann?"

Teeny shook his head. "Nope. How you doing?" he asked the other two.

"Where are you from, again?" Madison asked Teeny, as they all started to walk.

"I live in Florida," he said. "Just north of here. My grandmother wanted me to come here. She said I should learn something instead of wasting the summer surfing. So I figured I'd try it. I love fishing."

"We won't be fishing, will we?" Ann asked aloud.

"Not for dinner," Madison joked.

Will and Teeny both laughed.

By then, they had walked across a wide plank bridge over to the auditorium, where Leonard was gathering everyone. The four new friends sat down in a row together.

Leonard stood at the podium and ran through the list of camp activities. He passed around a calendar describing what they would be doing for the next two weeks. Then he clapped his hands together, smiled his crocodile smile, and cleared his throat.

"Now, on to the camp, groups."

Everyone in the audience shifted in his or her seat. The veteran campers pushed close together as if that would somehow ensure their being assigned to the same groups again this year.

"Okay, let's start over on this side of the room," Leonard said. He pointed to the row in front of him and counted off a group. "One, two, three, four, five —you will be Group A, for 'Alligators'."

Madison couldn't believe it. If he was just going to count off people like *that*, in the rows where they sat, then she and Will would end up in the same group.

It was too good to be true.

A second group was counted off, from a different row, and named Group B, for "Butterflies."

The third group was called C, for "Crabs" (although the kids in that group didn't like their name much). The fourth group was D, for "Dolphins."

Madison held her breath. There were only two more groups to be counted.

"One, two, three, four, five," Leonard said, pointing at Madison's row.

At Will's seat, he stopped counting. He didn't point to Madison.

"You will be Group E, for Egrets," Leonard said.

Madison took a deep breath. She thought she saw a look of disappointment on Will's face. Or was it just that she *wished* she had seen that look?

She knew she had a look of disappointment on her own face.

But before he started to count again, Leonard waved his hands in the air. "Wait!" he cried. "Go back for a moment. I miscounted."

He pointed to Madison.

"I should have said, 'One, two, three, four, five, and *six*,'" he said, now pointing his finger at Madison's forehead. "You should also be a part of the Egrets. Okay?"

"Okay!"

A smile spread across Madison's face. Her skin tingled with excitement and happiness. She was an Egret after all! Hurrah! Her entire body wanted to jump right out of the seat and high-five everyone in the room. But instead of making a scene, she scrunched down in her seat.

Lay low, Maddie, Madison told herself as she leaned back.

Will leaned over to Madison. "That's so cool," he said. "I was hoping we'd be in the same group. You know, since we're both from New York and all that."

"Yeah," Madison said. "Since we're from New York."

"Oh, my God!" Ann squealed. She leaned right over Will's lap, stretching all the way to Madison. "I told you we'd be together!"

"Excuse *me*," Will grumbled.

Ann grinned. "Sorry," she said. Madison thought maybe Ann was trying too hard, but she couldn't be sure. Ann seemed to be over the top about everything.

Madison glanced back to the seat where the Egrets' row started. She saw Teeny there, and another boy and girl she hadn't met yet.

The boy turned and looked over toward Madison.

"I'm Logan," he said. Then he turned to the girl at his side. "This is Laura."

"No, no. I am Suchita," she said. She spoke with an accent.

Logan had a head of thick, red-brown hair and brown glasses. He wore a T-shirt with a picture of a spaceship on it. He held up two fingers in a peace sign.

Madison tried very hard not to chuckle at him when he held up his fingers like that.

Leonard asked the different groups to go to lunch together and to spend the afternoon reviewing the camp schedule. That way, fellow campers would be able to get to know each other. From then on, those five or six partners would be the most important part of being at camp. Working together was as important as learning how to deal with sea life and turtle hatching.

The Egrets had lunch with the Dolphins and the Flounders (the last group to get chosen after Madison's). Madison was impressed by how much her camp experience had changed since the morning. Now she really *did* feel like a part of camp. It wasn't the same thing as Far Hills Junior High, with her cluster of friends, but it was the next best thing for now.

Stephanie came alone to pick Madison up when camp ended for the day. Dad was working. When Stephanie walked over, Madison introduced her to the rest of the Egrets. Then they said good-bye and walked back to the car.

Madison was grinning from ear to ear.

"Well," Stephanie said. "I don't have to ask how your first day at Camp Sunshine went. I can see it all over your face. *You* look like sunshine."

Madison giggled. "I know it's dumb. I was so worried about camp. But it was better than I could have imagined."

"So, tell me," Stephanie said.

Madison explained about the turtle wall and the aquatic center and all the other topics Leonard had covered during their introductory day.

"And . . ." Stephanie said.

"And?"

"What about the other kids?"

Madison shrugged. "Oh, they're nice. I think. I like my group."

"Mmmm," Stephanie mused. "I saw you smiling at that one boy."

"So?" Madison started giggling again. "I was not smiling. I was just being nice. That's what we were all being."

"Well, your dad will be very pleased to know you had a good day. He was worried about you and camp. You seemed so unsure when you arrived. And we want you to have the best summer ever."

"Thanks," Madison said. "I'm fine, really. I like Camp Sunshine way more than I thought. And we haven't even had the best parts yet."

Stephanie turned the car onto the main highway.

"I can't wait to hear about *those*," she said with a wide grin.

Chapter 7

Back at the apartment that evening, Madison's mind was still buzzing about her first day of Camp Sunshine. She called Mom to check in.

"Honey bear!" Mom gushed. "I've been waiting for your call. How was it?"

"You would not believe it, Mom," Madison explained. "They had live sharks, and we had to put on scuba gear and get into the tank with them—"

"What?"

Madison burst into laughter.

"As if, Mom," Madison said. "It was great, though. The camp is very cool. The people are nicer than nice."

"So, you'll make some new friends this summer

76

after all," Mom said. "See? And you were so worried."

"Yeah," Madison sighed.

"Hey, Aimee called up yesterday and asked if she could bring over her dog, Blossom, to play with Phin. We went over to the dog run in the park together."

"So, what's going on with Aim?" Madison asked. She felt one of her *I miss my friends so-o-o much* pangs coming on.

"Aimee is very, very excited about her dance performance," Mom said. "I told her I would definitely go to see her. She got me a ticket."

"Thanks, Mom, that's really nice of you. I wish I could see her perform."

"I know you do, honey bear," Mom said. "I'm sure all of your friends miss you as much as you miss them. Not to worry."

"By the way, I started a blog," Madison said. She gave Mom the exact address. "It's mostly for me and my friends, but you can check it out."

"Well, I will do that."

"What are *you* working on?" Madison asked.

Mom paused. "A little of this and a little of that. Budge Films asked me if I'd oversee this small documentary feature being directed by this incredible Chinese woman. It's a movie about the Great Wall."

"A movie about a wall?" Madison asked.

"The *Great* Wall," Mom said. "It's part of an even larger project Budge is sponsoring to find new voices in documentary film. My company is doing some big things, heading in new directions. Since my promotion, things have been getting very interesting."

"I know what that means," Madison said. "You'll have more and more work, right?"

"Well, I wouldn't say that," Mom said. "Maybe."

Madison couldn't keep track of Mom's film career. Mom always seemed to be working around the clock on some new project. Sometimes she filmed in the jungle. Sometimes she filmed inside caves. Sometimes she interviewed people for documentaries about historical figures. But mostly, she captured animals and wildlife on camera. That was the one thing Madison liked about what Mom did for a living. Madison knew that Mom's love of animals was, in part, where she'd gotten her own love of nonhuman creatures.

"I'm so glad you called tonight," Mom said. "I was just sitting here in my studio office with a cup of coffee and thinking about how much I miss you. Phinnie misses you too, of course."

"I know," Madison said, feeling momentarily choked up. "Give him a chew toy for me."

"Will do," Mom said. "And you keep me posted on that great camp adventure."

"Okay," Madison said. She puckered up and kissed the air, sending a long-distance smooch to Mom through the phone line. Then she hung up and reached for her laptop.

Madison had realized during the conversation with Mom that there was someone she had not spoken to in a very long time. She needed to talk to that person right now. Luckily for Madison, her keypal was online. All Madison had to do was send an Insta-Message, and *bing*! They were connected.

```
<MadFinn>: I MISS U!!!!!!!!!!!!
<Bigwheels>: r u in FLA now? I 4got
   when u were going
<MadFinn>: im here now camp started
   2day
<Bigwheels>: I wasn't sure :-/
<MadFinn>: did u get e-mail about
   my BLOG?
<Bigwheels>: OMG u have a blog 2?
<MadFinn>: :>) YEAH!!! JLY
<Bigwheels>: i have 2 read it
   NOWWWW
<MadFinn>: so ur @ camp too right?
<Bigwheels>: Y horses it's like a
   dude ranch place in Washington
   ILLI!!!
<MadFinn>: im gonna be watching
   turtle eggs hatch here
<Bigwheels>: well that's so kool so
   how r the other peeps @ camp?
<MadFinn>: OK
<Bigwheels>: just ok? :>)
<MadFinn>: there's one girl she's ok
```

and the guys are cute I guess
actually there was this 1 guy
named Will
<Bigwheels>: :>)
<MadFinn>: yeah he's QT but I
don't like HIM I like Hart,
remember?
<Bigwheels>: U can like both Y not?
<MadFinn>: U can't like 2 guys @
once NW
<Bigwheels>: IDBY!
<MadFinn>: Well u just can't.
<Bigwheels>: BTW, Reggie & I broke
up again
<MadFinn>: :>Z Y???
<Bigwheels>: b/c he sez he likes
someone else
<MadFinn>: he SAID that?
<Bigwheels>: Sort of but I don't
care. I don't like him n e way
<MadFinn>: Im sorry Vicki
<Bigwheels>: don't be hey IGG
<MadFinn>: now?
<Bigwheels>: I have 2 help my mom
clean the garage we're having
this end of summer yard sale
<MadFinn>: sounds good
<Bigwheels>: I'll read yr blog WBS
<MadFinn>: OK bye Ill WBS u 2!

Madison clicked to leave the chat room.

Her computer froze.

"Oh, no!" Madison wailed. "Don't do this to me again!"

Stephanie raced into the living room, where Madison had been sitting with the laptop exactly where it should be—on top of her lap. Together the pair tried to figure out what keys to press to reboot it correctly. But nothing seemed to work. That was when Stephanie wisely suggested that Madison go into Dad's office to finish her project for the day. Dad even had a high-speed Internet connection.

Dad's office was a room that was normally used as a sitting room or a bedroom. Madison stretched out on top of the bed and tried fiddling with her laptop for a few moments more. When that also failed, she turned on Dad's machine and crossed her fingers. Dad's laptop was a lot fancier than Madison's. His screen was wider. He had surround sound. It was like the Rolls-Royce of laptop computers—with Madison at the wheel. She hoped that she wouldn't press the wrong key or click the wrong button.

The first place Madison checked online was bigfishbowl.com's Bloggerfishbowl page listing. Had anyone blogged since the last time she'd checked? Madison was overjoyed to see postings from Wetwinz, BalletGrl, *and* LuvNstuff (aka Lindsay). She clicked on Lindsay's blog first and quickly scanned Lindsay's short profile before reading the rest.

Name: LuvNstuff
Country: US of A
State: NY
Gender: :-)
Favorite color: rainbow (I like them all)
Interests: theater, computers, READING!!
Expertise: Far Hills Spelling Bee Champ (for 3 yrs)

08-9
(I'm 6 whole hours ahead of Maddie & Aim & 9 hrs ahead of Fiona!)

I cannot believe I'm this far across the planet in London, England, and not just right next to you all. BOOHOOEY. So far things are going A-ok w/Dad. The plane over here was fun even though we had to wait @ the airport for three hours. (Or, as Dad would say using his best British accent "three bloody hours!") We're staying in the Notting Hill section of the city near Portobello Rd. and I am so totally going shopping here and yes, it's where they made that movie with Julia Roberts. How cool is THAT? I think we're going to see the Tower of London and Parliament and maybe take a cruise on the Thames. Dad has all sorts of sightseeing planned. It is wicked cool to be overseas though. I just wish u were all here with me. [BTW: Maddie great idea to do Bloggerfishbowl I wish I'd thought of it!] So far no cool or cute guys (no cracks, Aim) but I am still looking. I do have news to report however and that is in response to something Aim posted in her blog about Dan. I DID go 2 the animal clinic and did see him there BUT it was all good b/c he E-mailed me l8r that night to wish me g'bye on my trip. What do u think that means everyone? I am sooo curious 2 know if maybe there's a chance that he might like me too. E-me or post in your blog thoughts about this pleez. Maybe he'll even E-me again while we're in England. Maybe I'll send him a postcard from Buckingham Palace. LOL. Well, I have to go have tea and crumpets now. CU!

Aimee had posted a new blog, too. Madison started to laugh at it right away—even before she'd read anything.

08-9
My Top Ten Countdown of Reasons Why It Is :>(
to Be in Far Hills W/O My BFFs (insert drumroll here)
10. No one to pick on me for being a ballet addict
    ha ha
9. No one to sneak off to Freeze Palace to share a
    Brown Cow milk shake
8. No one home @ Fiona's big house (and it looks
    scary at night with that one porch light on)
7. Multiple sightings of Poison Ivy alone (RUN
    AWAY!)
6. Multiple sightings of Poison Ivy with drones (RUN
    AWAY FASTER!)
5. No Blossom walks w/Phinnie & Maddie (although I
    did walk w/yr mom, Maddie, and it was WAY cool)
4. Bigfishbowl chat room withdrawal

3. No one's shoulder to cry on when I don't see Ben Buckley around

2. Hart looks sooooo SAD w/o Maddie being around (seriously, he does!!)

1. I've decided that if I had to choose between my BFFs and my toe shoes (a tough choice 4 me, you know), I would def. pick . . . THE SHOES! J/K xoxoxox

"Hey," a voice called out from the doorway to Dad's office. "Who's in here hijacking my computer?"

"Just me, Dad," Madison said. "I'm stealing all of your secret files. You know how it is for us government agents."

Dad smiled. He kissed Madison's head.

"So, Stephanie tells me the first day of camp was a roaring success," Dad said. "Looks like you made it home in one piece. No shark bites."

Madison giggled. She was thinking of the joke she had played on Mom.

"Thanks so much for finding the camp, Dad, and letting me come down to Florida," Madison said.

"Anything for you, Maddie," Dad said. "Your laptop crashed again, huh?" He lifted its lifeless shell of a body off the bed close to where Madison sat. "Maybe I should take this to a repair shop."

Madison gulped. She was afraid of ever handing her laptop over to someone else. She desperately feared losing the Files of Madison Finn. Of course, once Dad reassured her that the files would be just fine, Madison allowed him to take it. He promised her that he would get the computer repaired within the week.

"I should get to sleep," Madison said, standing up and heading for the door.

Dad grabbed Madison's arm and pulled her close.

"Having you here is like a gift," Dad said. "Usually, these work things are endurance tests, but with Stephanie and you around—what's to endure?"

Madison smiled and headed for her own bedroom. She fished through her suitcase for a T-shirt to wear to bed, since the one from the night before had gotten orange juice spilled all over the front of it.

Brushing her teeth in the bathroom, Madison heard a loud sound. She turned off the running faucet for a moment to listen more closely. Then she heard it again.

Someone was yelling.

At first, Madison thought it was someone outside the apartment. It wasn't really that loud. But someone sounded angry.

Then Madison realized it was Dad and Stephanie. They were arguing about something.

It was the first time since their wedding that Madison had ever heard them argue with each other. She knew they got testy from time to time. Of course, every couple did that. But this sounded more than testy. It sounded more like the kind of argument that Mom and Dad had used to have, before the Big D had ever happened. Madison opened her bedroom door to see what she could hear. But the words weren't really audible, so she shut it again. She felt weird eavesdropping.

After a few moments, the argument must have ceased, because the yelling stopped. The only sound was the drone of crickets outside. Madison finished brushing her teeth, combed out her hair, crawled into bed, and said good night to her pink walls.

Click.

The light went off, and moonlight poured into the room. The curtains were still open. As Madison rested her head on the pillows, she closed her eyes to block out the light and tried to clear her mind of the day's events.

But instead of counting sheep to fall asleep, Madison counted pugs.

Each one looked exactly like Phinnie.

Chapter 8

On Tuesday, the Egrets gathered at one of the outdoor picnic tables at the ELC building and read through the outline of the day's activities.

"Oooooh, today we're seeing Manateeeeees!" Ann cried. She seemed to say everything in a really high-pitched squeal that made Madison's ears ring.

"Did you know those suckers were twelve feet long at least?" Logan said, reading information off the sheet. "That's the same size as a Rodan craft flyer on *Space Raiders*."

Ann giggled. "To you, everything is a relic from that show, isn't it?" she cracked. "Who watches that anymore?"

Logan took her comment in stride. "There are

those who understand and see the world as I do—and those who do not. . . ." He was making his voice sound like a robot's.

Suchita was laughing by now. No one wanted Logan to feel different from anyone else in the group, but it was hard—especially when he was doing the robot thing. Madison leaned over and begged Ann not to make another *Space Raiders* remark again for the duration of the two-week camp experience.

"Wait! Whoa! Did you see this point?" Teeny shouted. "The manatee eats more than a hundred pounds of aquatic plants a day! That is one big salad."

Madison glanced away from the group. She wasn't focused on the work sheet as much as everyone else was at that moment. She was way more focused on the fact that they'd be spending the day with actual, up close manatees.

The camp arranged to pick up campers from the ELC building and take them to a manatee-viewing area a few miles away, near the local power station. While they were on the bus—all six groups, from Alligators to Flounders—Leonard explained a little bit about the manatee-viewing.

"Now, we'll be standing down by one of the canals alongside the power station, where viewing is optimum. There are also tourists sharing our viewing space, so please be courteous," Leonard said.

Someone made a fart noise from the back of the bus.

"Very funny. I know who did that," Leonard said, wagging his finger at the back row.

The bus pulled into a tight parking space, where everyone got out and headed for the edge of the canal.

Madison found herself next to Ann. It was only day two, and she always seemed to find herself with Ann. Suchita came along, too. It was girls on one side and boys on the other at the start of the manatee-viewing. Madison kept trying to elbow her way over toward the boys. She wanted to stand next to Will.

He's just so interesting, she thought.

Madison tried to make excuses inside her head for why she was so drawn to this boy. She knew she should be missing Hart—not crushing on some new boy.

"Now," Leonard continued, "the locals work very hard to keep motorboats away from this immediate area in order to protect the manatees and their cubs. If you look right over there, just there, by that dock, I believe you can see a mother manatee right now. . . ."

Madison, Ann, and Suchita began to shriek when they saw their first manatee move through the water. It moved with such grace. Manatees had always seemed to Madison as if they were having a hard time in the water, with their blubber and their funnily shaped heads. But this creature was moving like a ballet dancer—sort of. Madison knew Aimee would have loved seeing it.

"My grandfather used to bring me here, too, when I was a kid," Will said as he stood near Madison and Teeny.

"Was he a fisherman?" Teeny asked.

"Nope," Will replied. "He was a conservationist."

"Oh," Teeny said. "Did he save birds and stuff?"

"And fish. And land, too. He made sure that estuaries were maintained for the life down here by the ocean and rivers," Will explained further.

Madison looked up at Will. She knew she was a little pie-eyed, but she liked hearing what he had to say.

"My grandfather once told me that when the Spanish explorers first reached Florida, they thought manatees were real, live mermaids. How cool is that?" Will said.

"Whoa!" Ann said. "That is cool all over!"

Madison wanted to cringe. Ann was being over the top again, waving her arms and smiling way too much. The boys snickered at Ann's behavior, but she didn't even seem to notice.

Madison looked away for a moment. The water was a little choppy because of a far-off motorboat, but the manatee seemed to ride in the wake, happier than happy to be there. Madison wished she could bottle the moment and bring it home with her—to be shared with his friends at a future date.

Most of the kids from the various groups stood silently along the guardrail, staring down into the water to catch sight of the manatee as it swam around. Then, from the bottom of the canal, a second manatee appeared, and then a third. Soon there were at least six, swimming around one another. Many of the campers pulled out cameras to capture the scene.

Madison was glad she'd brought her orange bag. She pulled out a mini-notebook to record her many observations.

Leonard stood in front of everyone and began to talk again about the survival of the manatee, and about manatees' characteristics.

"Who can tell me about the way manatees eat?" Leonard asked.

Someone poked her hand into the air and waved it around. It was Ann.

"They only have two teeth that can grind food—and those teeth wear out and fall out a lot," she said.

Will appeared impressed. "Wow, you're really smart, aren't you?" he said to Ann.

Madison frowned. *That was what he said to me.*

Ann modestly accepted Will's compliment and went right on talking about "manateeth" (which was what she called them) and other bodily facts and functions of the manatee. Madison wondered how Ann could have possibly known about how the animals held their breath, but she did.

"Does anyone know why manatees sometimes have a green glow in the water?" Leonard asked the group.

It was a tricky question that stumped even Ann. But Madison had a pretty good guess. She raised her hand.

"Is it because algae live on the skin?" Madison was answering Leonard's question with one of her own.

"Yes!" Leonard said as he pumped his hand in the air. "Now, what do they eat?"

"Mickey D's!" cried some boy from the back of the crowd, somewhere among the Crabs.

Everyone laughed.

"Although I am sure a manatee would just love a Big Mac, I'm afraid that's the wrong answer. But you get a C for effort," Leonard joked.

Madison knew the answer. It had been on the work sheet they had read back at the ELC. But she wasn't quick enough with her answer: about seven other kids had their hands up, eager to respond.

"Manatees eat sea grass," one kid said.

"And other aquatic plants," said another.

"Yes," Leonard said. "And what's important about manatees for Florida is that they eat up all sorts of floating vegetation and plants that can build up and clog the waterways."

Just then, a few of the manatees pushed through the water and made a splash. Everyone raced to see.

"Why do they hang out at a power plant?" someone asked.

"The water is always warm here," Leonard explained, "by the outflow pipes. Manatees can find warm water here anytime, especially in winter."

A loud, squawking bird flew overhead. Madison looked up. She saw an egret, too, in the air. Then she noticed another egret alighting upon the water in the canal several yards away.

"Look," Madison whispered to Will. "Our namesake."

Teeny heard what Madison said. "Go, Egrets!" he yelled. The birds flew off.

"Good one," Logan grunted. "Zarloff of planet Zoltan would have *loved* you."

"What?" Will had no idea what Logan was talking about. No one did. Logan's geekiness quotient was skyrocketing with each new comment that came out of his mouth.

Suchita, however, laughed out loud in a gentle way at everything Logan said. Madison noticed that although she didn't speak much, she had a great sense of humor. Suchita reminded Madison a little of Lindsay, except for the not talking. Lindsay was a bigger-than-big talker.

"Here's something for you to mull over," Leonard said. "Before we head back to the ELC, see if you can't observe more of the manatee's anatomy. I know it's hard to see much in the murky waters here, but manatees have some interesting body parts. See what you can find out."

"Like what?" a kid asked.

"Like fingernails," Leonard said.

"So, do they get *mana-cures*?" Madison joked under her breath.

Ann heard her. "That's hysterical," she told Madison, slapping her on the shoulder and faking an outrageous, nasal laugh.

Will had heard Madison's dumb joke, too. "It *was* funny," he admitted in a low, low whisper so that only Madison could hear what he said.

The groups stood by the manatee-viewing area for another half hour or more. Then they loaded back on to their buses and headed for the ELC again. Parents would be coming back soon to pick everyone up for the day.

Once again, Stephanie showed up solo to get Madison.

Back at the apartment, Stephanie grilled Madison on day two at Camp Sunshine. She asked about the cute boy, of course, but Madison tried to avoid that subject. When Dad still had not returned by dinnertime and Stephanie couldn't get him on his cell phone, she and Madison decided to order take-out Mexican food from a restaurant down the street.

After the food arrived, Madison noshed on quesadillas while Stephanie devoured chicken with mole sauce.

After dinner, Stephanie asked if Madison wanted to play a card game or maybe Scrabble, but Madison wasn't in the mood. Instead, she escaped to Dad's office. She hadn't written in her blog for more than a day, and she needed to go online—now.

She'd been in the office for only a few minutes when she heard the front door slam.

Dad.

She started to get up to rush into the other room to say hello and tell Dad all about camp that day, but then she heard Dad yelling. She stopped in her tracks.

"Come on!" Madison heard someone shout from the other room.

The voices were like ones she had heard the night before, only louder, faster.

"Please keep your voice down," Madison heard Stephanie say more than once.

This time, Madison could hear everything clearly. In fact, it was hard *not* to eavesdrop. She leaned against the door frame and pressed her ear to the door.

"I didn't plan this," Madison heard Dad say. He sounded frustrated, angry, and tired. "This client is very important. My cell battery died. I promise you—"

"Save it," Stephanie growled. "You should have found a way to call. Your daughter is here staying with us."

"I know. Maddie understands."

"That isn't the point, Jeff," Stephanie said.

The sound of their voices dipped a little bit, so Madison pressed closer to the door. She could hear only bits and pieces of their dialogue.

Suddenly, she heard a door opening.

"Maddie?" her dad's voice called.

Madison shuffled backward and threw herself on top of Dad's bed, pretending to be immersed in her work, or her laptop. She clicked a button, but nothing came on. Dad's laptop was unplugged! She panicked: she needed to look busy. She just knew her dad was coming down the hall.

The door opened slowly, but it was Stephanie standing there, not Dad. What was Madison supposed to say? A million things raced through her mind.

Then she noticed Stephanie's eyes. They were pink-rimmed, as if she'd been crying. The two of them just stood there and stared at each other blankly for a moment before Dad came into the room, too.

"Hey, Maddie," Dad said.

"What's going on?" Madison asked.

Dad put his arms around Stephanie's shoulders and pulled her close.

"We're okay," he said. He kissed the top of Stephanie's head as he addressed Madison. "Look, I'm sorry I was late tonight."

Stephanie took a deep breath. "I'm sorry, too, Maddie. I'm just a little tense these days," she explained. "It's work. . . ."

"Okay," Madison shrugged.

She knew something was up—way up. But she didn't ask any more questions.

Chapter 9

Dad acted super nice for the rest of the evening. After he apologized for missing dinner, he even invited Madison to use his laptop again.

As Madison got herself set up at the computer, Dad slinked out of the room. Madison entered his password and clicked on the Internet browser key.

SERVER BUSY.

The bigfishbowl server had gotten busier than busy these days, with all of the new games and features offered on the site. The company had promised an update, but that hadn't happened yet. While Madison waited for the server to come back online, she thought about all the crazy things that had happened since she'd arrived in Florida. This was the most jam-packed (or, as Gramma Helen would say, strawberry-jam-packed) vacation ever.

Beeeeeep. Beep. Beep. Beep.

Madison looked at the screen and grinned. She was finally online.

After checking her e-mailbox—empty? Bummer! —Madison moved to some other areas of her favorite interactive site.

First stop: Bloggerfishbowl. There were brand-new posts there from Fiona, Aimee, and Lindsay, in that order. But Madison completed her own blog entry before checking out the other ones. She didn't want to derail her train of thought from the day at Camp Sunshine.

08-10

I never thought I'd say this but: MANATEES ARE BEAUTIFUL. I think we should put a bumper sticker on our car back home that says that. At the end of the day, Will told me that he thought Ann and I were the smartest girls at the camp. I don't know how he knows that, since he hasn't even met all the other girls there, but that's what he said and I liked the compliment. BTW for those of you in the pitch black dark here: Will is this guy at Camp Sunshine who could be a model or a TV star. He is that cute. And he's also smarter than smart, obviously. The truth is, I can't believe I'm actually wasting brain space thinking about him. Am I crazy? I want Hart, right? I mean, Hart is mine, right? If I had to do a total comparison of Hart and Will, I just know Hart would be declared the winner. He would have to be. No contest. So I need to put this Will guy right out of my head. Now.

BTW: I think you should aim really, REALLY high in London, Lindsay, when it comes to guys, that is. Like . . . Y don't you try to find Prince Harry? LOL. And a special shout out to Fiona from moi: pleez write more. I miss u. :>). GTG.

Madison clicked POST. Then she hit the BACK browser button and selected another blog page. She clicked on Fiona's name, and a blog page popped up with images of little soccer balls around the edges. Fiona was getting good at design—and at computer games. Madison figured it was the Egg influence. She read the blog.

08-10

Have u ever ridden on Space Mountain? I hadn't ridden it even though I lived here 4 so long. Well, it ROCKED. That's what Chet kept saying. He waited on line and rode it SEVEN times. I only rode twice. Otherwise I would have thrown up. :>) We're off tonight for my old neighborhood. I'm sleeping over @ my old BFF Debbie's house and I can't wait. I wish u all could meet her. She sounds exactly the same as when I left, but I'm still nervous about seeing her and the old group. Deb told me that everyone knows I'm coming and this guy I used to like whose name is Julio (remember, Maddie?)—well, he's around and he knows I'm coming. He told Deb he wanted to see me. OMG. Ok. So no one can tell Egg about that one, ok? I feel a little guilty even though I know that's dumb b/c Julio is really just a friend. Anyway, it's nice that Julio wants to be friends again, right? Meanwhile, my mom and dad keep talking about how much they miss California. Dad says he misses his old job out here. When Uncle Ron told them about an old house, Dad instantly started talking about how he could renovate it. I don't think anyone is serious about moving back here--it's all just talk--but I still can't help thinking about it. I love Far Hills and everything, you guys know that. But I love it here too. I just had forgotten how much.

Madison reread Fiona's entry *twice*, but she didn't want to think too hard about what Fiona said. How could Madison swallow the idea that her newest BFF would move back to her old home, all the way across the country? That would never happen! It just *couldn't* happen.

Aimee's blog was next. Madison began to read—slowly

08-10

OMGOMGOMG Did u guys read Fiona's blog? F: you can't move back to CA!!!!!!!!!! Hello? You have us now and we need 2 stick 2gether. OMG I don't like it that ur so far away. It's bumming me out. BTW: dance is good. Well, it's better than good. Someone from the local paper has been coming to rehearsals and apparently they want to do a human interest piece (whatever that is) on ME!!! I sort of laughed it off @ first but then Mom said it was a chance to show my stuff. I guess the local paper is profiling all sorts of kids our age. My fear: IVY will get her own page, too. Can u imagine how weird that would be? What is HER special talent? I can just see her red-haired 'do on the front page with a caption: "Local Girl Wins Everything, Gets All the Guys, and Never Gets Zits!" LOL. But seriously, things here are looking pretty rosy-rosy. No, I have not seen Mr. Ben Buckley, but that's cool b/c dance takes up like 9 hrs a day and I don't have much time 4 n e thing else EXCEPT this most excellent BLOG. Don't forget, Fiona, ur NOT moving. Just wanted to say that again because I could. ;>)

Madison grinned at Aimee's plea to their BFF. Then she turned to Lindsay's page to read. Of course, Lindsay had attached photos, including one taken at the Tower of London (where she was pretending to put her head on a real, ancient head-chopping block) and one taken at their hotel (where she was, in fact, sipping from a teacup). Lindsay looked cool posing in a foreign setting. Madison noticed that in one of the photos she was even wearing a blue T-shirt (with a dog's face on it) that Madison had lent her.

08-10 (Tuesday afternoon)
It's later in the day & Dad and I are headed to the Tate Gallery here in London and I CAN'T WAIT! I want to see the Rosetta Stone. Do you guys remember reading about that in school this yr? It's this stone where all language

originated. It has the three original languages on it. I think.
I need to do some more research on it. And of course I feel
like I need to see it, considering I am the biggest reader in
our class. Well, I don't mean to brag, but reading is the one
thing I'm pretty cool at. I've already read three books while
I've been on vacation (mostly on the plane & at bedtime).
And I read that book u loaned me, Maddie, the one called
Sixth-Grade Glommers, Norks, and Me. Liked it a lot. And of
course I read the new Harry Potter! They have these huge
displays for the book here, too, just like in the U.S.A. Maybe
I'll see J. K. Rowling on the street somewhere. How cool
would that be? Dad let me go to this very hip bookstore
near where we're staying. I spent an hour in there. He
had to drag me out. :>) But I miss u all sooo much. Do
u miss me? I promise 2 send more pictures. Did I say I
miss u? :>&

Madison couldn't help smiling. She felt as if all of
her friends were right there in the room with her.

Just then, the computer screen went blank.
Madison gulped.

Was she causing every laptop she touched to crash?

A moment later, she realized the computer was
fine. It was bigfishbowl—again. The message
flashed: SERVER DOWN.

Madison closed the windows that showed
each of her friends' blog pages. Then she opened
a word-processing document. The blog entry
she'd composed was for everyone else's benefit, but

the files were for Madison Finn's eyes only.

Of course, she'd have to save any file she created to Dad's hard drive. But she could e-mail it to her e-mailbox later—when Dad got her orange laptop up and running again.

 Hit the Beach

Rude Awakening: Slow and steady wins the race, unless you're talking about Internet connections or love connections. Sigh. My two weeks at Camp Sunshine would be a lot more fun if:
   a) my laptop didn't keep crashing
   b) Dad and Stephanie weren't fighting
      all the time
   c) I didn't miss Hart s-o-o-o much.

"Madison! It's for you!"

Madison stopped typing and looked around the room. The clock said it was a little after nine. She hopped off the bed and stretched her arms overhead, shook out her hands, and blinked a few times.

Stephanie poked her head into the room.

"It's for you," Stephanie said, handing her the portable phone.

Madison's stomach flipped. It was late. Was it Mom? Aimee? Or maybe Hart?

She laughed at herself. *Hart didn't even have her dad's phone number.*

"Oh, it's someone from Camp Sunshine, I think," Stephanie said before she disappeared through the door again.

That made Madison's head spin even more. *Someone from camp?*

Was it Will?

Madison's throat constricted. She raised the receiver to her ear.

"Maddie, am I calling too late?" a voice hollered.

It was Ann. *Of course.*

"I wanted to call you, because I was surfing online and I found your name using Google."

"You *what*?" Madison asked. Her heart sank. Had Ann discovered Madison's blog? No, she couldn't read that. It was password-protected on bigfishbowl.com. What had she found?

"I googled you," Ann said. "I was sitting here looking up stuff online about manatees and turtles—you know, for camp—and then I put in your name, and it came back with all these hits."

"What hits?"

"Well, your name is listed under the staff of the Far Hills Animal Clinic. How cool are you to volunteer for that?"

"Oh, yeah," Madison said, still kind of dreading hearing about whatever else Ann may have uncovered.

"And I found your name in the credits for the Far Hills Junior High school Web site. If you surf around that site, there are pictures of you and your friends, too."

"Really?" Madison's voice shook a little bit. Even though it was only Ann who was revealing all of this, and even though the stuff she had found online was pretty harmless, something about Ann's discovery bothered Madison. It was as if she'd shone a flashlight onto some secrets and now they were illuminated for the whole world to see. Madison made a quick mental note *not* to mention Ann by name—ever.

"So, you called to tell me this?" Madison asked her fellow camper.

"Uh-huh," Ann said. "I just thought it was so cool."

"So, you're done looking up my name now, right?" Madison asked.

"I guess," Ann said. "It's fun seeing where you go to school and who your other friends are."

"Yeah, well, it is kind of late now," Madison said, trying to cut Ann off.

"I'm sorry," Ann said quietly. "You sound mad."

"I'm not mad," Madison said. "I just have to go. That's all."

"Oh. Well, I'll see you tomorrow."

"Tomorrow . . ." Madison said, her voice trailing off.

She hung up the phone, a bit stunned by the exchange. Of all the people in the world who could have called her, she hadn't expected Ann. And she hadn't expected Ann to learn so much about Madison's life during one Internet search.

Madison went back to the computer and reread her short (and thankfully private) file. Then she pressed SAVE. The blog was great. The school Web site was great. But Madison knew that the best place to talk about her real feelings was in these private files.

Yawn.

Madison opened her mouth wider than wide.

Yawn. Yawn.

She couldn't stop yawning, which clearly meant that at that moment she needed sleep more than anything else. Her eyes ached from looking at the computer, reading all those blogs, and doing Internet searches.

It had been a lo-o-o-ong day.

So, with a click and a *zap*, Madison turned off Dad's computer and turned herself off, too. She crawled onto the bed and whispered good night to the moon just as she had the night before.

And then Madison whispered good night to Aimee, Fiona, and Lindsay, too—long distance, of course.

ELC 18th Annual Scavenger Hunt

DO YOU KNOW YOUR
FLORIDA WILDLIFE AND HABITATS?

ITEM/CREATURE TO FIND	BASIC POINTS	EXTRA-CREDIT NOTES AND QUESTIONS (2 points each)
❏ 1. Small lizard	2	What color is it?
❏ 2. Palm tree	2	What was on the ground nearby?
❏ 3. Butterfly	3	Where was it?
❏ 4. Pelican or ibis	3	Was the bird eating?
❏ 5. Rotten log	3	What did you find on the log?
❏ 6. Ferns or sea grape	3	Name two other types of vegetation that you see.
❏ 7. Crab	4	Size?
❏ 8. Mangrove	4	What else was in the area? Make a list.
❏ 9. Three different rocks	6	Find a fourth rock that sparkles.
❏ 10. Three different shells	6	Find a piece of mica.

ITEM/CREATURE TO FIND	BASIC POINTS	EXTRA-CREDIT NOTES AND QUESTIONS (2 points each)
❏ 11. Set of animal footprints	4	Identify the animal.
❏ 12. Three types of insects or spiders	6	Can you find a spiderweb?
❏ 13. Blue jay or scrub jay	5	What sounds did it make?
❏ 14. Small fish	5	What kind?
❏ 15. Alligator	15	Why aren't you running away?

Chapter 10

The third day at Camp Sunshine, which was Wednesday, turned out to be quite sunshiny indeed. Stephanie dropped Madison off outside the ELC. Dad was off at work again.

Once inside, Madison immediately bumped into Will and Teeny. Their parents had just dropped them off, too.

"Hey," Will said when he saw Madison.

"Hey," Madison said, smiling.

"Are you ready for this?" Will held up a yellow sheet of paper with a chart on it.

Madison nodded. Everyone had been given a list to review the previous night. The groups would team up for a camp scavenger hunt today. Of course, she had gotten the list just like everyone else, but for some reason she had glanced at it only that morning, on the drive over, and she hadn't looked at it closely. The night before, she'd been more focused on feeling homesick. Although she liked camp so far, she missed her friends.

"Just tell me: how are we supposed to find all this stuff?" Will asked.

"Yeah, and what's a scrub jay?" Teeny asked.

"How come 'Find three bugs' counts as one thing to do and not *three* things to do?" Logan asked.

"And 'find three shells' and 'three rocks,'" Suchita added. "Why so many?"

Madison laughed. "I really can't believe they put 'alligator' on the list. Where are we going to see one of *those*?"

"Yeah, right," Teeny said. "I see one of those and I'm so outta here."

"The alligator must be a joke," Will said as the three of them sauntered inside with the rest of the campers.

"Hey, guys, wait for me!" Ann said chasing everyone inside. She'd just arrived. Immediately, she came over and stood right next to Will, arms waving all over the place as she explained how that morning she'd almost overslept and almost lost her cat and just missed being super late for camp.

"Whoa," Teeny cracked. "Take a breath."

"Sounds like a pretty gruesome morning," Will joked.

Madison couldn't help chuckling. Ann sounded silly. But she kept right on talking.

"Anyway! I am so ready for this hunt," Ann said. "I think that our group has the best chance of winning, don't you? Because it's only been a day, but we are all really tight already, right?"

Madison felt herself wince, just a little bit. It had been only three days at camp and already Ann was convinced the Egrets would be friends forever.

And why did she keep touching Will's shoulder?

"What were you guys talking about just now?" Ann asked.

"Hmmm. Not much," Teeny replied.

Teeny and Will started to walk toward one of the round wooden tables in the entry area of the ELC. Leonard had posted signs with the group names on the tables: Alligators, Butterflies, Crabs, Dolphins, Egrets, or Flounders. Suchita and Logan were already seated at the Egrets' table.

"Let's sit next to each other," Ann suggested. She linked arms with Madison as they walked over to the table.

Madison didn't put up any kind of fight, but Ann's clinginess made her uncomfortable.

A moment later, thankfully, Leonard clapped his hands to get everyone's attention, and Ann broke loose.

"Everyone!" Leonard cried. "As you know, we have a big, big day today. So let's get organized.

Please take your seats at the tables if you haven't done so already."

Madison glanced around at the other teams. She wished Ann were on the Butterflies or Flounders instead of on her team.

"Aren't you excited? Aren't you?" Ann said, a little too enthusiastically, tugging on Madison's T-shirt. She was too close, Madison thought.

Way too close.

Leonard reviewed the items on the list. "Now," he explained. "Some of these things may seem a little impossible to find, but trust me—it's all out there in the natural habitats. You are allowed to search for any of the items anywhere at the learning center."

Then Leonard passed out maps.

"You will see on the map that there are defined areas to search. This includes a sandy beach area, a small pond near a wooden bridge made from old logs, and a mangrove swamp. But you can look anywhere at ELC if you need to. Remember that. *Anywhere.*"

One kid from the Crabs' table raised her hand.

"So what do the points mean?" she asked tentatively.

Leonard explained how the teams were supposed to keep track of items on the list, checking them off as they found them. "Keep notes on what you see, because I will be collecting every team's notes in order to score the results," he insisted. "And

113

go for those extra-credit points. They will make all the difference."

"This sounds like way too much fun," Suchita whispered to Madison.

Madison wasn't exactly sure what that meant. How much fun was too much? There was no such thing, she thought.

Logan tapped out a drumbeat on the table. "Know what? We are winning this. I don't lose, and *we* will not lose."

Teeny agreed. "You're so right, Logan. This scavenger hunt is *ours*." He threw his hand out and placed it on the center of the table.

Immediately, Ann slapped her hand on top of Teeny's. Then Suchita put hers down; and then Logan and Will after that. Madison laughed at her team's determination. She liked it.

"Well?" Will asked. "Are you in or are you out, Mad Dog?" That was the strange nickname he spontaneously gave to Madison.

Sheepishly, Madison put her hand on top of Will's hand. "I'm in," Madison said. It felt so awkward to be touching Will—even though it was just a handshake pileup. Did this count as holding hands?

"Go, team!" Teeny cried. The hands went into the air with a cheer, and Madison felt as if she had been in the locker room before a big game.

The teams scrambled to leave the room as Leonard declared the official start of the hunt with a

114

sharp whistle. His parting words were, "Have a good hunt, and be back by noon."

The Egrets hustled outside toward the mangrove swamp with everyone else. It was the closest spot on the map—and it would have many of the items on the list.

Leonard and some of the other counselors joined the kids as they all marched toward the same places.

"Maybe you should split up so that you aren't all in the same area at the same time," Leonard suggested. He disappeared back into the ELC.

"So what now?" Teeny asked.

Madison shrugged. "Let's pick a place where no one else is headed."

They moved toward the small beachfront. It turned out to be a smart move. No one else was there.

"I see a shell! No, I see two . . . no, *three*! Wait, there are, like, a hundred shells here," Ann said. She raced around as if someone had wound her spring up and then just let go.

Madison noticed the boys giggling at her antics.

Suchita, who was taking the hunt very seriously, pointed to a grove of sea grape set back from the shoreline. "That's on our list, too!" she said.

"And there's a pelican," Logan said, pointing to the water.

"And an alligator!" Will yelled.

Everyone shrieked. Then Will cracked up and fell

onto the sand in mock hysterics. Madison smiled. He'd played a good joke.

"Now we need to find an egret," Madison suggested as they lingered on the beach.

"Why?" Teeny said. "It's not on the list, is it?"

"Because we *are* the Egrets!" Ann cried.

Madison couldn't believe that Ann was the one and only person in their entire group who understood. That was a major fluke.

After leaving the shore, the Egrets headed to the mangroves, since the other groups had left by then. Along the pathway, Logan picked up a few rocks, and Ann found a rotting log. They examined the log for creepy-crawlies, moss, and extra points (of course). As they were taking notes and observing, two of the camp staffers came by to congratulate them on their hard work. One of the staffers snapped a photograph.

After an hour went by, nearly all the items on the list had been found. They'd seen both a pelican and an ibis, or at least Will thought they had seen one. No one was really sure if they could tell one bird from another. The bird-watching lesson was happening on a different day.

"So what's left?" Logan asked, looking over the list.

Ann was quick to point out all the things they'd missed. "Well, we didn't see a crab," she said, sounding rather bossy.

"Yeah, we did," Teeny said. "It was on the beach. Wasn't it?"

Ann looked at everyone. "We can't say we saw it if we didn't *all* see it."

"Why not?" Suchita asked. "I believe Teeny."

Ann put her hands on her hips. "Look, I don't want to be a downer, but we have to play this fair, or we won't win."

Will rolled his eyes. "What else did we miss on our list?"

Ann spoke right up again, reading down through her list and notes. "Well, we saw about twenty of those little lizards. We found a set of animal tracks. . . ."

"Dog tracks," Madison pointed out.

"Are you sure?" Logan asked.

"Yes," Madison said right away, even though she wasn't entirely sure. In fact, she wasn't entirely sure about any of it. How could six total strangers be expected to agree on all of these things?

"I think we saw the scrub jay, right?" Ann said. "You know, there's a petition to make the scrub jay the state bird."

"Huh?" Teeny asked back. "What does that have to do with our scavenger hunt?"

"Maybe we'll get extra points for knowing that little factoid," Ann suggested.

"She's right," Madison said.

"Factoid?" Teeny said, repeating the word with a laugh.

"Okay. What about the alligator?" Suchita asked.

Ann laughed out loud. "That was just a joke! Will even said so."

"What if it wasn't?" Madison asked.

Everyone stared at her.

"Huh?" Ann said. "Of course it was a joke."

"Madison, you don't think the camp expected us to see a real, live alligator, do you?" Logan asked.

Madison shook her head. "No, but . . ."

"But *what*?" Ann asked.

Madison gazed off into the distance. She knew that Leonard would not have put the word "alligator" on the list if he hadn't really expected it to be found—by someone, somehow. This was the best brainteaser ever.

She wanted to solve it.

"What if . . ." Madison thought aloud, "what if there really is an *alligator* somewhere around here?"

"And what if he's hungry?" Will teased.

"That is so *not* funny," Ann said.

"Seriously," Madison continued, "this is worth fifteen points. We should think about it for a minute."

"All we have is a minute," Teeny said. "We have to get back soon. It's almost twelve."

They started back on the path toward the ELC building. Will and Teeny were tossing around the little rocks they had collected near the beach. Suchita was in charge of the shells. Logan had stuck a dead beetle in his pocket—for proof that they'd seen the biggest bug. Ann had their master list in hand. She kept stopping to scribble new notes.

Madison wondered what more she could be writing. Who had made her the group leader?

As they all walked along, a cluster of kids from the Butterflies and the Crabs scuttled past. They laughed as if they knew something no one else did.

"Hey," Teeny called out to the two groups. "Did you see the alligator?"

"Ha-ha; very funny," retorted one of the other boys.

"There's no alligator!" a girl said with a laugh.

Will turned around to catch Madison's eye, as if to say, *See, no one else thinks there's an alligator either, so why don't you just give up on the idea already?*

But Madison wouldn't give up.

She let the other groups pass and walked on behind her five teammates, surveying the path, checking the brush for signs of a real alligator. Was there one hiding in the pond that everyone had missed? The gator *had* to be somewhere. But where? Madison glanced up at the main ELC building. In a window of one classroom, she saw a miniature whalemobile.

She stopped short.

"Wait! That's it!" Madison screamed out.

Will and Ann turned around. The rest of the

119

group raced back to where Madison stood.

"I know where the alligator is," Madison declared with a huge smile on her face. "I know! I know! Drumroll, please . . ."

"Come on! Just spill. Where is it?" Logan asked. "We only have a few minutes before time's up. . . ."

"Remember that place we saw on the tour? The room with the stuffed owl and the dolphin posters and . . ."

"The giant plaster alligator!" Will said.

"Wow," Suchita said. "I didn't even think of that! Leonard didn't say it had to be real. A fake alligator. Of course! You are so smart, Madison."

Madison blushed at the compliment, especially at the idea that it came from someone who hardly knew her. "Thanks, Suchita," she said.

"You are a total genius," Logan said.

Ann nodded in agreement, but for the first time all day she didn't say much. "I wish I'd thought of that," Ann muttered under her breath.

"Yeah, well," Will said. "You didn't. But that's cool. We're a team. All for one and one for all, right?"

Madison started to laugh. "A team," she said. *Was she still blushing?*

"Shhhhh!" Teeny whispered. "I see the Flounder and Dolphin teams coming down the path."

The six Egrets stopped talking and tried to act cool as the other camp kids passed by. Once the other group had walked on (with suspicious looks on their faces, because they knew *something* was up), Ann took charge again.

"So, now that we know we will win for sure," she said in her most authoritative voice as she checked one of the last items off the list, "let's celebrate."

"Not so fast," Madison said.

"Yeah, don't count your eggs before they hatch," Teeny said.

"Chickens," Suchita said, laughing. "Don't count your chickens."

"Oh, yeah," Teeny giggled.

Madison, Will, and the others laughed again, too. Everyone was feeling a little looser now. They were this close to the finish line—and to winning.

What could be better than that?

As the groups approached the main building, Leonard and the rest of the camp staff welcomed back the scavengers with a loud round of applause. He told everyone that the staff had been observing the groups as they proceeded through the different areas of Camp Sunshine—from the mangroves to the pond to the beach. Then he asked a few random questions about animal habitats. Before the hunt, only a few kids could have answered the questions. But now everyone knew the answers. The scavenger hunt had been a success on many levels, and now everyone understood a lot more about Florida wildlife.

Before the time came to review the scavenger-hunt sheets, Leonard and the camp staffers dismissed everyone for lunch. Madison and her fellow Egrets could hardly eat their turkey sandwiches and tangelos. They wanted to know who had won—for real.

"Attention, everyone!" Leonard shouted. "We have our results. Would everyone give me your attention, please?"

The groups sat patiently as the answers were read for each question. By the third question and answer, it was clear that the Butterflies, Crabs, and Flounders were all in trouble. They'd forgotten to cross off "lizard" or "rocks" or one of the other items on the list. Meanwhile, the Alligators, Dolphins, and Egrets were running neck and neck—until the question about fish came up. The Dolphins had said they had seen a fish, but hadn't been able to identify it correctly. Madison's group had named carp as the fish in the pond—and so had the Alligators.

And so, the race for first place was between the Alligators and the Egrets.

It all came down to the last question.

"I want to congratulate the Alligators team," Leonard said. "You guessed correctly that the alligator on the list was the sculpted one in the nature room. Of course, I figured maybe you guys would

122

guess correctly, considering your team's name. . . ."

The Alligators high-fived each other in celebration. One of the members cried out, "Number one!" with his finger held high in the air.

"Wait!" Ann spoke up. "We guessed that, too—"

Madison grabbed Ann's arm. "Hold on," she said. "Look at Leonard. He's not done yet."

A smiling Leonard waved at the Alligators. "I'm afraid you weren't the only team to find the alligator on the list," he said.

The Alligator team members stopped celebrating, just like that. They looked deflated.

"Our Egrets team also answered correctly," Leonard said.

"So it's a tie!" one of the Alligators cried out.

"Not exactly," Leonard said. "There was the extra-credit question, don't forget."

Madison felt her whole body turn cold. *The extra credit question?* They'd forgotten to fill that in. She wanted to sink through the floor. *How could they have forgotten something so important?*

"Oh, no!" cried one of the kids on the Alligators. "The extra-credit question!"

The entire Alligators team looked upset.

Leonard, however, was still smiling.

"Egrets," he announced proudly, "you are our scavenger-hunt winners! You correctly answered enough of the items on the list—which, with your extra-credit notes, win today's hunt. Congratulations!"

The other campers and staff members let out a roar and started clapping like mad.

Madison turned to her teammates, who were smiling from ear to ear.

"How did we do it?" she asked aloud.

Will shook his head. "We got all the answers."

"But—" Madison said. "We didn't fill in the last part, the extra-credit part. We only put down where the gator was found—"

"No," Ann corrected Madison. "At the last minute, I saw that we forgot the extra credit. "I filled it in."

"You?" Madison cried with disbelief. "Whoa. That's amazing. You're—"

"Yeah, well . . ." Ann said with her all-knowing tone. "I told you we'd win. And I was right, right?"

Madison bit her tongue. Ann *was* right. They reached out and shook hands, but Ann quickly pulled Madison toward her for a squeeze.

"I told you when we met that we would make the best friends, didn't I? And if it wasn't for you and me, we wouldn't have gotten half the stuff on the list," Ann gushed. "See? And so I was right about that, too."

Madison grinned. She wasn't sure how she felt about her friendship with Ann just then, but she did know she was happier than happy to win.

Later in the day, when Stephanie and the other parents and guardians came by to pick up the campers, the sky opened up. A hard, pounding rain poured from the gray clouds that had been threatening for part of the morning. It lasted only for a few minutes, but everything outside, including Madison and the rest of the Egrets, got drenched.

Still, it was a case of perfect timing. The rain had held off long enough for the Egrets to win the prize—a tin trophy emblazoned with six words:

CAMP SUNSHINE
SCAVENGER HUNT
FIRST PLACE

Madison felt proud. She'd worked together with her teammates—even Ann—to win. Camp seemed like a positive adventure now, certainly more positive than it had the day before.

She couldn't wait to tell her BFFs all about it.

Chapter 11

Thursday morning before heading over to the ELC, Madison sat in front of Dad's computer monitor. Her laptop was still acting up, although Dad had promised it would be repaired soon. But since he continued to let Madison use his machine, there was no problem.

She logged into bigfishbowl.com and headed for the Bloggerfishbowl area, signed in with her password, and clicked the start key: NEW ENTRY.

Madison had been thinking all night about what to write. She had a lot to say. Her fingers raced across the keyboard.

08-12 early morning!
OMG OMG OMG I am so XCITED we won this contest today. We =

126

me and the other peeps in my group: Teeny, whose real name is Anthony, Suchita, Logan, Will, and Ann (who is really clingy but I'll tell u more about that l8r). N e way, we're called the Egrets. That's a cool name, right? Don't make some crack like we're for the birds LOL--because we are truly THE BEST of everyone. We had to search for all this stuff on the beach today and in the woods, too. OMG again--am I making any sense? I just can't believe we won something. I wish I could scan in a picture of this trophy and show you--winning first place in anything is such a cool feeling. Actually, I wish I could show u what all the other Egrets look like, too. It's so weird becoming a part of this new group and having 2 get along w/everyone. We are ALL so different. These peeps are nothing like u guys. :>(But I'm dealing. Of course I miss Phinnie a little bit, too. No one 2 snuggle with @ night . . . boo hoo. SO . . . how r u? F: how's sunny CA? L: Do you have tea in the afternoon in London and did u c & take yr picture w/a beefeater yet? That's a question fm. my dad, actually. A: W ^ in FH? Have u seen Hart a lot? He hasn't e-mailed me yet even tho he promised. I'm a little bummed. Maybe I should send him this blog link and my password to read this. No, on second thought, maybe I shouldn't. Then he would find out how much I really, really do like and miss him. Yikes! And don't you DARE say that 2 him, Aim, ok? How's the dance practice coming? Did yr brothers come home from their summer vacations & jobs yet? Oh well, I just heard this HUGE clap of thunder and Dad sez I should get off the computer so I will. BFN! Post yr blogs ASAP!!!

Madison hit POST and waited for Dad's computer to acknowledge that everything had gone through correctly. She was about to log off, but then she realized that she had not surfed the Bloggerfishbowl area of the site to see if her BFFs had made any posts of their own. So she ignored Dad's warning and looked up Aimee's, Fiona's, and Lindsay's blogs. As luck would have it, all three had posted something the night before.

Madison skimmed Aimee's first.

08-11

True or false: Ivy Daly is not only mean but she's dumb. Answer: What do you think?!

I went over to the pool yesterday to go swimming w/my mom during their open lap swim time. And I saw Hart there (yes, Maddie, he wuz looking very tanned and I must admit--cute with a capital C). So I was in the water doing the crawl and Ivy and her drones must have come in when I was swimming & not looking. Next thing I knew, I bobbed out of the water & saw Ivy talking 2 Hart like he was her BF (not best friend but BOY friend) or something. She is so full of herself. Maddie--Hart TOTALLY blew her off like more than I've ever seen him do b4 so u have NOTHING 2 worry about. But I wished I had a camera to take a picture of what happened. It would be super good 4 blackmailing her!! LOL. Okay--that's all from home. Off to dance class again. I'm getting really good at pointe. I wish you could all c me--but I'm making a video so don't worry--maybe u'll c me when u get home and we can have another slumber party. OK so blah blah buhbye.

Madison reread Aimee's blog and had another good laugh about Ivy. It was good to hear that Hart was still "in like" with Maddie, or at least seemed to be. The thought of Poison Ivy squirming with embarrassment after Hart's rejection gave Madison almost as much pleasure as winning the scavenger hunt had.

She clicked on Lindsay's blog next. Lindsay had posted a smiley face on the top of her entry.

08-11 (Wednesday, nighty-night from London)
Maddie when I read one of yr BLOG pgs I wuz thinking hard about that fortune u got on Ask the Blowfish b4 we left. Didn't it say something like WILL BE YOURS FOREVER or something like that? Well, isn't the new cute guy @ Camp Sunny (or whatever) called WILL????? Maybe that's what your fortune means. Like WILL will be yours forever. If not that is just too much of a weird coincidence doncha think? What do Fiona & Aim think?

BTW: 2day we went on a double-decker bus and took a tour. It is really tiring going all over sightseeing but I liked Picadilley (I think I might have spelled that wrong?) Circle (or maybe it's square). We did some shopping too. My Aunt Mimi would be so proud--I bought this incredibly funky pair of earrings. I know u will all want 2 borrow them--except 4 fiona, who doesn't wear dangly stuff. :>)

I miss u guys and Far Hills and even Dan (Who has not sent me another e-mail yet but my fingers r SO crossed.) It is way harder 2 crush on someone long distance, right??? I really hope Dan remembers me after vacation. P.S.: no, still no QTPIES 2 crush on here. Not yet BUT I'm waiting. More fingers crossed. Oh well. LYMTCCIAMC (which means: Love ya more than chocolate chips in my Aunt Mimi's cookies). A bazillion hugs 2 everyone wherever u are.

Fiona's blog was the last one Madison read. And it was a long one.

Her friends were really getting into the blog-writing thing.

08-11
Good-bye Disneyland, Hello Northern California! We're in Los Gatos finally at my Uncle Ron's HUGE house. He is still talking about that other house he saw and Dad and Mom are STILL joking about renovating it. Whatever--Dad is always making these big plans that never turn into anything big. I'll keep you posted if we decide to stay here (LOL--Like that would ever happen--we only just moved away)

SO . . . tomorrow is the big day when I meet up w/my old friend Julio again. You were right, Lindsay, I'm a teeny bit nervous. Okay, I take that back. I'm TOTALLY nervous. Aimee said it doesn't have to be a big deal, but I don't know. Isn't it? After all, Julio is the one guy I ever really and truly kissed--and we kissed more than once. Well, not that much more, but still, you know what I mean. And it's only been a year or so but I wonder if he's changed. He had grown five inches the summer before I went to Far Hills. He could be a giant by now. My friend Paige says he's definitely cuter than he was.

OK. Yes, yes, YES--I DO FEEL GUILTY. I know I should be thinking about Egg and not some old boyfriend. Well, not that Julio was ever really a boyfriend--but you know what I mean. I never imagined I would feel like this.

Half the reason I feel SO guilty though is b/c Egg has been Insta-messaging me and e-mailing all week so far. I mean, he knows I'm seeing my old friends so it's all good, isn't it? Am I the worst person on the entire planet? F-I! F-I! F-I! (I have to forget it or I'm doomed.)

All my old California BFFs seem exactly the same as when I left here. But I feel like I changed a little. Or maybe I've changed a lot? And we played a pickup game of soccer (my old pals and teammates) in the park and I thought I was going to M-E-L-T. It doesn't seem like it's that much hotter than Far Hills, but it is. And this morning I checked the Weather Channel and it's only supposed to get HOTTER out here. Luckily, Uncle Ron has central AC. Whew. But hot out here is bad when it's dry, which it is right now and that means there could be wildfires. Scary stuff. Chet's funny though. He says he misses getting fried in all this heat. He's so happy to be back. His old best friends James and Reynold and he went biking together and he had a blast. He also got a major sunburn. (Meanwhile on the Weather Channel, Maddie, the guy said there's a hurricane going to hit Florida. Is that TRUE? Aren't you right on the coast, Maddie? LMK!!!)

Sorry this is such a long, lo-o-ong blog entry but I had a lot to say. Of course I miss you three. Like Maddie always says, life is just way, WAY better knowing you BFFs exist. Peace out!

And I will def. keep you posted on you-know-who. But don't tell Egg no matter what--you hear me, Aim???!

Madison couldn't believe Fiona's blog entry. She had to reread it just to make sure she hadn't missed something. She wanted to reach right into her computer and grab Fiona and say *"What are you thinking going to see Julio?"* Madison knew that even if Fiona said she didn't like her old crush anymore, she probably didn't mean it. It wasn't because Fiona was lying, exactly. But how could she possibly like Julio *and* Egg at the same time? That was like saying she liked Coke and Pepsi equally. There was no way.

As Madison surfed around bigfishbowl, Stephanie came to the door of Dad's office, which was ajar. She knocked gently.

"Maddie?" Stephanie whispered. "Oh, I don't want to disturb you with your files," she said.

Madison motioned to her to come inside. "I'm disturbable. Wait. Is that a real word?"

"I forgot to tell you that your mom called last night," Stephanie said, looking forlorn. "I should have said something, but . . . I was preoccupied. I forgot. No excuses."

"It's okay," Madison said. "I'll just call her back now."

Stephanie still looked upset. "She misses you," Stephanie said, her eyes looking a little bit pink. "She told me to tell you that."

"Is everything okay, Stephanie?" Madison asked. She quickly thought again about the fight she'd heard the other morning. It was the second argument Dad and Stephanie had had since Madison had arrived.

"Oh, Maddie," Stephanie shook her head gently. "Don't worry. I'm just a little emotional these days."

"Are you sick?"

"Not exactly."

"Then what's going on?"

Stephanie plopped herself down on the large club chair near the desk where Dad's computer was set up. She took Madison's hand in hers and breathed in deeply.

Madison wasn't sure she wanted to hear this. Her head began to spin, like the Tilt-a-whirl carnival ride. What was Stephanie going to say? Were things not working out in the marriage to Dad? Was someone really sick of somebody? Was Stephanie sick of Madison?

"It's my job," Stephanie said plainly. "I got cut."

"You mean fired?" Madison asked.

Stephanie nodded. "After all those years in the same place . . . and it's hit me hard, that's all.

Sometimes mornings are hardest. I don't know why. Because I don't have a job to go to—maybe that's it."

"Wow, losing your job, what a drag," Madison said, trying her hardest to sound comforting. "Is Dad okay about it?"

"Your father is always okay when it comes to me," Stephanie said. "It's just that . . . well . . . we had plans, and this changes things."

"What kind of plans? Changes what?"

Stephanie paused. "I should really let your father speak to you about all of this," she said in her steadiest, calmest voice.

"Okay," Madison replied, not sure what all the secrecy was about.

Stephanie kissed Madison on the top of the head and walked out of the room. She looked just as distressed as when she had first come in, but Madison told herself not to worry. Stephanie was good at taking care of herself. She'd get over those blues.

After Stephanie left, Madison remembered she owed Mom a phone call. She picked up the receiver and dialed Far Hills.

Mom picked up on the second ring.

"Hello, Mom?"

"Maddie? Where are you? I called but then I didn't hear back from you and—"

"Sorry, Mom," Madison assured her. "Nothing to

worry about. I was just super busy with camp and all. Then Stephanie told me you called. . . ."

"I heard on the TV that there's a major hurricane bearing down on the Atlantic. They think it may hit Florida. Have you heard anything more?"

"Not more than that," Madison said.

"Okay, then things aren't as bad as I thought," Mom said.

"They're not bad at all, Mom," Madison said. "I made new friends. I even sort of like someone: this boy named Will."

"What happened to Hart?"

"I still like Hart, of course," Madison explained. "But . . ."

Mom started to laugh. "Okay, you don't have to tell me everything. Shouldn't you be at camp right now?"

"We're leaving in a little while," Madison said.

"Oh, honey bear. I'm sorry for overreacting. I guess I just miss you too much."

"That's okay, Mom," Madison agreed. "I miss you too much, too."

They both giggled.

"What's on the agenda for today's camp session?" Mom asked.

"Someone's coming to lecture us about turtles. Then on Friday we're going on a pontoon. We're learning how to bird-watch. And next week it's all about the turtle nests and—"

"Wow, I'm impressed," Mom said.

Madison spied the digital clock in the office. It was time to go.

"It's getting late. I'll call you again soon," Madison said quickly.

"Or E me," Mom reminded her. "You can always E me."

Madison hung up the phone, powered down Dad's computer, and shut off the light in the room. She grabbed her orange bag and headed for Stephanie's car. When she got there, it was clear that Stephanie had powdered her nose and around her eyes. She looked a lot less puffy.

The drive over to the ELC was long. Traffic on the one access road to the center was blocked for nearly a half hour. At nine o'clock, when Madison was supposed to be lining up for camp activities, she still sat in the air-conditioned SUV.

Madison hoped she wasn't too late for the start of the camp day. It had taken her awhile to get used to the place.

Now that she liked it, she didn't want to miss a thing.

Chapter 12

When everyone had gathered together in the Seahorse Auditorium, Leonard stood up at the microphone and introduced the morning's special guest.

Her name was Myrtle Shelly, which was just right for someone who wore a sweater with a large turtle-shell insignia on the front, turtle-shaped earrings, a charm bracelet decorated with miniature turtles, and shoes with bright green, clip-on turtles. Madison guessed that Myrtle must have been at least seventy years old. She'd been watching turtle nesting habits along the coastline for decades. But alongside all the turtle trinkets, there was something about Myrtle that seemed . . . *familiar*. Madison couldn't put her finger on it.

Before the presentation, Logan and Teeny started whispering. Madison wanted in on the joke, but she could barely hear them. Ann was in the way. She sat between Madison and the other members of the group like a roadblock.

"When I woke up this morning, I was so glad to see it was not raining hard again, weren't you?" Ann asked.

"I guess," Madison said, trying to avoid any kind of real conversation. She couldn't believe that the second she arrived at camp for the day she had ended up paired up with Ann again. How had that happened?

"I talked to Will on the phone last night," Ann said in a low voice.

"Oh," Madison turned to her, eyes wide. "That's nice."

"He called me to find out what was going on at camp today. He thought we were supposed to bring show-and-tell things. I guess he figured I would know what we were doing."

"I guess," Madison said. "Um . . . We should really try to pay attention now, right?" Madison pointed in the direction of the lectern.

"Oh, yeah, yeah, sure," Ann said.

Myrtle stood up at the lectern.

"Hello, my dears," she said, her voice deep and strong. She didn't need a microphone. She walked around the stage as she spoke. "Before I start to tell you all my turtle tales, I want to clarify one thing that I've been clarifying for years: my name, Myrtle Shelly, does *indeed* sound like turtle shells. You didn't hear wrong. And I didn't plan it that way, but it's been good fun all these years, so enjoy it. Now that we've gotten that settled . . ."

The crowd of campers applauded; some giggled. Myrtle showed the first slide. It was a picture of a beach overrun with turtles.

Madison felt Ann lean in.

"So, did *you* have a good night last night?" Ann whispered.

"Huh?" Madison couldn't disguise the annoyance in her voice.

"Did. You. Have. A. Good. Night?" Ann repeated, emphasizing every single word.

"Shouldn't we be paying attention?" Madison asked curtly. She leaned on her opposite elbow and sighed.

"Okay, I get it," Ann said. "You don't want to talk."

"No, I just want to listen," Madison said, quietly indicating the stage. "Don't you?"

Ann turned the opposite way. She was pouting a little bit; Madison could tell.

Up on stage, Myrtle wasn't saying much to start. She let the photos do the talking.

Thankfully, Ann finally focused on the presentation, too.

Clicking through a sequence of slides, Myrtle rattled off each turtle fact with a dramatic flourish. She started every sentence with a flamboyant, "And did *you* know . . . ?" and ended every sentence with a joke. Madison laughed at most of them. Her dad would have loved them all.

"Did you know that Ridley, the smallest sea turtle, weighs about a hundred pounds, but the leatherback weighs almost thirteen hundred pounds? Now, that's a lot of turtle soup!"

The campers laughed, too, happy to learn as much as possible about the turtles before the following week. That was when all six groups would head for the beach to see *actual* hatchlings appear from the turtle nests dotting the coast. It would be the payoff camp experience, after two weeks of hard work.

"Now," Myrtle explained in her croaky voice, "the Indian River coast is home to many different breeds of nesting turtles. We try to be as welcoming and protecting as possible."

Madison took it all in. One day, she hoped to be able to be as smart as Myrtle was, standing up in front of other people, able to share her knowledge of animals and the environment and . . . to make a difference. She thought back to her plane ride down to Florida, about sitting next to Walton, who called himself Wally. She remembered one of the many important things Wally had said: *If you just stop*

and listen, you can change the world, you know.

Up on the screen behind Myrtle and the lectern, a slide flashed showing a large turtle with a dark, rubbery-looking shell.

"This is the leatherback turtle," Myrtle explained. "It's the most active of all sea turtles. It dives thousands of feet into the water. . . ."

"Remember that scene from *Finding Nemo*?" Madison heard Teeny whisper to Logan. He went on to recall the scene in the animated movie in which a large group of turtles traveled through the ocean.

"*Dude,*" Logan grunted back, imitating one of the turtles from the movie.

Both boys laughed. Madison laughed to herself, too. Logan was funny; almost as funny as Egg. Madison wondered what Egg was doing just then. Was he swimming at the pool with—*sigh*—Hart? Madison still pined for her BFFs a little, but she realized that the Egrets were good friends to have around, too.

Even Ann.

"The turtle you are looking at now," Myrtle continued, pointing to the screen and trying to get everyone's attention, "is the green turtle. There have been sightings of up to fifteen hundred nests each year, although most nest on islands in the Caribbean Ocean. Many years ago, I had the good fortune to witness one of the green turtles' nests with my husband, Walton, a researcher and writer. . . ."

All at once, the sound of ten dozen pinball machines went off inside Madison's head. How could she have been so dumb? This was Myrtle, the same Myrtle that Walton, the man from the plane, had told her about. Duh! This was *the* Myrtle. Madison had always believed that coincidences were very good luck, but this was a doozy. How could it have taken her so long to see the connection?

Madison glanced over in the half-darkness of the Seahorse Auditorium and saw Ann scribbling notes. She was always taking notes on something. Just beyond Ann, Madison's eyes caught Will's eye. He was staring at her.

And then he smiled.

Madison froze.

It was just a smile—an ordinary smile. But everything about it made Madison's stomach flip-flop.

She quickly turned to face forward.

How long had he been staring at her?

Without thinking much about what had happened, but needing to confirm that it had indeed happened, Madison shifted her body slightly and looked one more time.

Will was still staring.

Madison froze again, but this time she was looking right at him. After a moment, she looked away again.

Flip. Flop.

The last reptile Myrtle put up on screen was the

most important turtle of all—at least for Camp Sunshine's purposes. This was the turtle Madison and her fellow campers would be searching for along the coast.

"Ah, the mighty loggerhead," Myrtle said as she pointed to the screen. "It's named for its rather large head and jaws. It crushes heavy-shelled clams, crabs, and other animals for food."

Although she didn't turn to look (she wasn't sure she could ever turn to look that way again), Madison heard Will and Teeny laugh about something. Madison hoped it was the turtle they were laughing at—and not her. There was no particular reason to think that that was true, but she was feeling just a wee bit paranoid. Was it Ann's influence? For some reason, Madison felt self-conscious about everything just then.

The lights went up and Myrtle continued her talk. Now she asked campers to tell her what *they* knew about loggerhead turtles.

A kid down in front raised his hand.

"I know that they have heads shaped like logs," the kid said.

Everyone laughed out loud.

"Well," Myrtle's voice was deep, but gentle. "I suppose you might say that," she said. "Anyone else?"

"I know that the loggerhead is on the endangered-species list," another kid grunted.

"Yes, yes, very good," Myrtle said. "Did you know

that there used to be millions of sea turtles in our oceans? But because of the demand for sea turtle meat, eggs, shells, leather, and oil, their numbers have been greatly reduced. It's sad, but we can help change all that."

A few other kids raised their hands, and added their own points. Naturally, Madison wanted to raise her hand and say something, too. She'd surfed the Internet for more than an hour the night before just to learn a few cool turtle facts of her own. But the whole eye-contact thing with Will had turned Madison's brain off, not on. Sitting there, she couldn't recall a single fact.

Madison didn't even utter a peep when Ann aggressively nudged her and said, "Madison, say something; I know you want to; you know a lot about turtles," in that squeaky voice that had—in only three days—driven Madison crazier than crazy.

But it was too late to participate. Myrtle was no longer looking for contributions from the kids. The presentation had ended. Leonard was back up at the microphone, leading a round of applause for Myrtle—and the turtles.

"Brilliant," Leonard said, clapping his hands together. "And campers?"

He looked out at everyone, urging them to clap louder. Madison leaned backward ever so slightly so that she could look behind Ann's head and spy on Teeny, Will, and the others during the round of

144

applause. Madison caught a glimpse of Will's shaggy hair. He had on a T-shirt with a license-plate design on the front and sleeve. She'd noticed it when they sat down. Now she could just barely see it. The letters *ILUVDOGZ* were pictured on the license plate.

Madison smiled to herself. Will would probably like Phinnie, wouldn't he?

"Now, campers, if you would like to introduce yourselves to Mrs. Shelly," Leonard said as everyone was dismissed, "you will have an opportunity to do so at our lunch. Please follow the other groups into the dining area."

Madison shuffled into the dining room with the rest of the Egrets. Thankfully, she didn't have to deal with Ann. She must have gotten the hint, Madison mused. Logan was standing there talking to her. Suchita and Teeny were joking around together, too. That left Madison and Will next to each other in the lunch line.

It was hard not to giggle, standing there. Madison felt awkward and more self-conscious than ever. She couldn't stop thinking about—or seeing inside her mind—Will's green eyes staring back at her in the auditorium. Her stomach still had not recovered. What with the nervous flip-flops caused by Will's staring and the pangs brought on by missing her BFFs, Madison had a total case of indigestion.

As they stood there, *not* speaking, Myrtle Shelly breezed past. Madison turned to look just as Myrtle walked by. And she nearly collided with Myrtle's shoulder. But the near miss gave Madison a chance to say a proper hello.

"Oh, n—n—no," Madison stuttered, "Mrs. Shelly, I'm so sorry."

"No blood," Myrtle joked as she smoothed her sweater with a free hand. "Any injuries?"

"No," Madison replied.

"Well, then, no doctors needed."

"Thank you so much for your speech," Madison gushed, tripping over her words. "I feel like I already know you. Of course, I do. Well, sort of . . ."

"Come again?" Myrtle stuttered. "I'm not sure I understand you, dear."

"Well, the truth is, I do know some things about you from before today. I know that your grand-daughter and you have the same name."

"Oh?" Myrtle's eyebrows went up.

"You see, when I came here from New York, I sat next to your husband, Wally, on the plane."

"Aha!" Myrtle cried. "So *you're* the fine, funny young girl he was telling me about!"

Myrtle took Madison's hand in her own. Her skin was softer than soft. She held on tight as she contin-ued speaking. "Walton told me he hasn't had such an enjoyable flight home in a dog's age. And he flies at least once a month, so that's really saying some-thing."

"Well, he was totally nice to me," Madison said.

She was still wondering why Myrtle described her as a fine and *funny* young girl. What was so funny about Madison?

"Yes, you are a real sweetheart, aren't you? I would love to chat, my dear, but I'm starved. Toodle-ooooo!"

Madison nodded. "Yes. Toodle? Oooo? Um . . . thanks!"

And just like that, Myrtle dashed off.

"You *know* her?" Will asked Madison as soon as Myrtle walked away.

Madison nodded proudly. "Sorta."

The server presented Myrtle with a lunch tray, and she sidled up to the counter for a helping of macaroni and fruit salad. Will wandered over to the tables where everyone sat.

Of course, Ann grabbed the seat right next to Will. It was a key body block. Madison ended up in the chair next to Suchita and some other kid from the Crabs.

But Madison didn't mind.

She had a better view of Will from where she was anyway. It was a good time to get a little distance, to let her stomach flips and flops subside. It was one of those sweet moments she'd have to write about in her files.

And to make things even sweeter, Madison even caught Will staring a few more times during lunch.

Chapter 13

After dinner Thursday night, Madison went online before heading to bed. To her delight, she discovered her keypal online.

<MadFinn>: W^?
<Bigwheels>: 22cool that ur online @ the same time as me AGAIN this wk. that NEVER Happens twice, right?
<MadFinn>: nvr say nvr
<Bigwheels>: so how's camp :-/
<MadFinn>: I like this guy Will, :>P 2day was just nuts
<Bigwheels>: WDYM nuts?? Details, pls.

\<MadFinn\>: well yesterday we ended
up touching
\<Bigwheels\>: KISSING??!
\<MadFinn\>: LOL yeah right
\<Bigwheels\>: hmmmmmm
\<MadFinn\>: and 2day he was SATRING
at me forever
\<Bigwheels\>: satring?
\<MadFinn\>: I mean STARING IDK am i
making 2 big a deal out of this?
\<Bigwheels\>: r u & Hart O&O?
\<MadFinn\>: OCN! No way!!! But I
think I do like Will a little bit
I can't stop thinking about him
that's bad right?
\<Bigwheels\>: {:>$
\<MadFinn\>: I know I know *megaguilt*
\<Bigwheels\>: ur not married. LOL!!!
\<MadFinn\>: LOL let's change the
subject how's yr summer???
\<Bigwheels\>: I got a tattoo
\<MadFinn\>: What?!!!
\<Bigwheels\>: LOL J/K
\<MadFinn\>: :)
\<Bigwheels\>: *yawn* my life is the
same as always
\<MadFinn\>: which is great how's
reggie
\<Bigwheels\>: *yawn* don't like him
anymore
\<MadFinn\>: Since when???

<Bigwheels>: Tuesday

<MadFinn>: What?

<Bigwheels>: OMG U r soooo gulliver
today

<MadFinn>: u mean gullible?

<Bigwheels>: oops yah well reggie is
supercool but he's leaving for
his camp in a week and I'm sad
;>Q

<MadFinn>: That's soooo how I felt
leaving Hart in Far Hills ;>Q

<Bigwheels>: My brother is @ a
special camp this month for
autistic kids

<MadFinn>: I haven't checked yr blog
18ly

<Bigwheels>: I haven't written in it
in weeks

<MadFinn>: Y?

<Bigwheels>: I dunno I think I
started getting these feedback
comments fm peeps who saw it and
read it and I felt weird that
they knew about me does that make
sense?

<MadFinn>: yeah it is weird
putting stuff online that's sooo
personal. I like how it's an
easier way 2 share than e-mail
but it's so

<Bigwheels>: so weird somehow

<MadFinn>: yeah ur right I guess u
  have 2 b careful what u say
<Bigwheels>: I just decided maybe
  it's better 2 keep my brother's
  stuff private & also not talk
  about myself so much since my mom
  freaks that some internet stalker
  will find me she's still a little
  bugged out about us being keypals
<MadFinn>: she is???
<Bigwheels>: a little bit but that's
  cool. She's cool.
<MadFinn>: <brrrrrr> LOL
<Bigwheels>: HEY How cool would it
  b if we ALL went 2 the same
  camp--u, me, reggie, and Hart?
  Should we ask our moms next
  summer? I so wish we could meet
  in person!
<MadFinn>: we would have the best
  best time
<Bigwheels>: TOTO

Talking to Bigwheels was better than eating ice
cream. Madison felt yummy all over. And by the time
they said their fourteenth good-bye and Bigwheels
went *poof*, Madison wasn't feeling quite as guilty
about her burgeoning crush on Will.

It was only a two-week crush anyway, right?

Madison logged off and then curled up in bed.

After lying awake in the dark for a half hour, her thoughts bouncing from Hart to Will and back to Hart again, Madison finally got the bright idea to count turtles in her head.

By the count of seventy-three loggerhead turtles, she was asleep at last.

"It's raining again?" Madison groaned when she woke up on Friday and looked out the window to see puddles everywhere.

"Afraid so," Stephanie said. She poured Madison a cold glass of orange juice. "It's been at it for hours and shows no signs of stopping. I actually called your camp to see if it was canceled. But no, it's still happening. They just want everyone to bring a rain slicker."

"A slicker?" Madison said. That sounded *so* kindergarten.

The original camp plan for the day had been to go bird-watching on a pontoon boat. Now that trip would be moved to week two.

Much to Madison's surprise, Dad was still in the apartment that morning. His own business meeting for that day had also been rescheduled.

"I'll drive you over to the ELC this morning," Dad said. He had a scruffy beard. He looked tired.

"Sure thing," Madison said, sounding less than enthusiastic.

"I'm happy to take her over, Jeff," Stephanie said. "I know you have some phone calls to—"

"I told you I've got it under control," he said.

"It's okay, Dad. I know you're busy."

"No," Dad said firmly. "I'm not busy today."

"Jeff," Stephanie said in a low voice. "We'll be together this weekend. No worries. You don't have to—"

"I *know* we'll be together this weekend," Dad snapped. "You don't have to talk to me like that, Stephanie."

"Like what? I was just—" Stephanie started to say.

Dad cut her off. "Let's not get into this again, Stephanie," he said coldly.

"Daddy?" Madison spoke up. "I think she was just trying to . . ."

"I *know* what she was trying to do," Dad grumbled.

"You know everything these days, don't you?" Stephanie said, shaking her head. "But I don't. I don't know what you want from me, Jeff."

Stephanie walked out of the room. There was silence for a moment. Madison felt weird about breathing, let alone speaking. But she did.

"Dad? What was that about?" Madison asked. "Are you and Stephanie okay? Because the other day she told me there were some things going on. . . ."

"What did she say?" Dad asked with a frown. He looked up at the ceiling and bit his lip. Then he looked away. "Oh, Maddie," Dad said. "I wish you didn't have to hear this."

"Hear what, Dad?" Madison said. She put her hand on his back to make him turn around and face her. "It all sounds familiar to me," Madison said.

"No," Dad said. He shook his head. "Aw, I don't know. Let's go."

Madison was afraid to ask for more details. She knew for sure now that something (and a not-so-good something, at that) was happening between Dad and Stephanie. But Dad didn't seem to want to talk about it. And Stephanie had disappeared into their bedroom with her coffee mug.

What was going on?

There would be no answers that morning. Rain slicker in hand, Madison followed Dad to his car, and they drove over to the ELC.

Madison checked her reflection in the backseat mirror. With all the rain, the air felt hotter than it had the days before, and it left a film all over Madison's body. Her skin was part rain, part sweat, and all . . . *gross*. She dreaded the thought that Will would see her looking like that.

For some bizarre reason, an edgy Dad decided to accompany Madison in to the ELC—even though Madison begged him not to. Camp had been going on for a week; no one had their parents bring them inside anymore. To make matters worse, Dad insisted on meeting Madison's camp friends.

Everyone was mingling in the front when she and Dad entered.

Teeny and Ann were sitting talking. Ann saw Madison right away and waved. Half the other kids in the room were sopping wet, as though they'd been standing in the rain for a day. All the wetness, combined with the body heat, made the room downright steamy, even though the ELC's air conditioner was running.

Madison didn't see Will anywhere. A part of her was grateful—she didn't want Dad to embarrass her in front of him. Another part of her was disappointed. She had wanted to see what Dad's reaction would be.

"Are you going to introduce me to your pals?" Dad whispered. "Or are we going to stand here like totem poles?"

Madison wanted to shrink down to the size of a minnow. *Pals? Totem poles?* Sometimes Dad could be so corny.

"Hey, Mad Dog," someone called out from behind Madison. She whipped around and saw Will standing there.

He was there.

Madison saw Dad's eyebrows shoot up. "Mad Dog?" he repeated, a little suspicious of the name. "Is that *you*?" he asked Madison.

"Don't ask," Madison said, giving him the brush-off. "Long story."

"Is this your dad?" Will asked right away. He gave Dad a flat little "Hey, what's up?" wave.

Just then, Teeny and Logan came over to see what was going on. After that, Leonard and other camp staffers walked in.

Dad knew it was time for him to go.

"Yup, I can see you're busy," he said calmly. He turned to leave. Madison was pleased with Dad's getaway. No major embarrassments had been incurred.

But then Dad surprised her. He turned on his heel, took five long strides over to Madison, and grabbed her shoulders. Dad kissed her—*smack!*—on the cheek. "Love you, sweetheart," he growled. "Don't forget your slicker."

Madison saw Teeny laugh at the word "slicker." She felt her skin flush with mortification. This was her most embarrassing moment to date—which was saying a lot, considering the number of times Madison had been embarrassed in her very short life span.

Of course, there was nothing surprising in the way Dad spoke to Madison, as if she were in first grade, not seventh. But nothing could counteract the embarrassment.

After Dad's departure, the day went by pretty quickly, although the group spent most of the time indoors. Madison didn't actually spend a lot of time with Will, though. She ended up hanging out with Suchita and Ann most of the time. Guys gravitated toward guys, girls toward girls.

All of that didn't mean that Madison ever let Will out of her sights. By the time the day ended and they'd played a game of "ocean charades," completed an underwater word puzzle, and helped to reorganize a part of the nature room, including touching up the paint on the plaster alligator, Madison and Will had had a few conversations.

Nothing seemed to connect with as much meaning as it had the previous day. Madison wondered if maybe her attraction to Will were just a blip. After all, the connection to Hart was much stronger. And it would last much longer—wouldn't it? What would her BFFs have said?

By the time camp was officially dismissed and Dad came to pick Madison up, all she could think about was getting home to check the blogs. Why were the only people who could truly have helped Madison get through moments like this now located so many miles away? It didn't seem fair.

And why was it still raining so hard?

Back at the apartment, Dad didn't seem to mind when Madison decided she'd rather log on than play a game of Scrabble with him. Ordinarily, she loved playing games with Dad. He usually let her win. But today, the need for blogging was greater than the need for a board-game fix.

After an hour, the rain still showed no signs of letting up.

The first blog Madison checked was Fiona's. But Fiona had not written in a day or more. Madison wondered why—and then skipped over to Aimee's and Lindsay's blogs, respectively. Aimee's was short.

08-12

Maddie you NEVER have 2 worry about Hart. 2day I was @ the pool and I saw Ivy AGAIN trying to put her mitts on him and he TOTALLY blew her off again. The best part was the drones, who were there with her highness-- Phony Joanie and Rose Thorn. I think her status as Poison Ivy has made her downright poisonous. Then l8r I was getting a diet soda at the vending machine and he came over and talked to me for like 10 mins. He never talks 2 me. But I think the way he figured--I was the next best thing 2 Maddie since Maddie is soooo far away. At least that's what I THINK was going on. Or maybe I was just a good reason to ditch the drones. Remember when he used to attempt niceness with them. Not anymore. C U. Actually I should say something else. b/c we don't C each other online! Duh!

Lindsay's blog was *not* short. It was long and juicy, too, packed with zany stories about London.

08-12 (Thursday)

OK r u ready to LAFF out loud REALLY LOUD? This is the blog entry where I have to admit that even though we've been sightseeing like crazy and I've had tea every single day and crumpets, too with clotted cream, which sounds kind of gross but is really the opposite of gross. YUM! Like whipped cream only sweeter and thicker. And for all of your information (and upon BFF request) I posed for photos inside one of those red phone booths, with a beefeater (believe it or not!), on a cruise ship traveling quite fast toward Greenwich, outside St. Paul's Cathedral, and inside (way down) the Parliament station of the underground (aka subway). There the walls look like they're reinforced with steel twenty feet thick. Did you know that there are no garbage cans in England like there are here--on the streets, that is? There are all these precautions here because of bombings in public places. Just thinking about bombs makes me nervous of course but they have a lot of police around here so it's cool. It's just as many police as we see at Grand Central Station in New York. Everyone is just trying to be safe and I feel safe. Today we went off for half the day to Hampton Court. I took the day trip with Dad and his friend--this old, whiskered "bloke" (Dad says). Duff is named after the character Macduff in some Shakespeare play. Do any of you know that play? Don't ask me!--weird, right? The train was not so long a ride and I laughed most of the way. The Duff guy is SO funny and he talks like a real English guy. Well, probably because he is one. :>P Good one, Lindsay! Anyway Duff gave me this little pamphlet with a list of British expressions. I just know you will all LOVE them. Here are some of the best ones I like. You know them probably from all those Louise Rennison books that Egg's sister gave you, right, Fiona? She always says "ginormous"

and "chum-ettes" and stuff like that. I think I'll use one off this list in an English paper when we go back to school. LOL.

> That's aces=It's great
> don't give a toss= don't care
> Shut your gob=Shut up
> snogging=kissing
> Sod off=Go away
> splash out=go all out

Do you think I'm learning how to fit in in London--like a crash course in becoming someone I am not? HA HA. That's what it feels like sometimes and we are staying in these hotels that have minibars and Dad lets me eat whatever I want. I must admit I have eaten at least ten chocolate Flakes. It is the best chocolate EVER. I know I will be covered in zits by next week. But that's ok, right? Because no one will ever see me except for Dad and tour guides and tourists from Japan and the USA and they don't count. It's not like DAN is here or n e thing<:-)

I have been waiting for a day or more to see yr blog, Maddie. Where did it go? I know Fiona hasn't written either. What's the deal, guys? I'm writing all the time and so is Aim. Come on!!!!! And pleez keep yr fingers crossed that next wk maybe I'll luck out. If I sing "Someday My Prince Will Come" really loud, maybe he'll just show up at the hotel. I wish but I think maybe London is just 4 sightseeing. LOL. Then again, what if a warty frog shows up and offers to be turned into a prince if I kiss him? Wait--what am I talking about?!!!

Help!!! I better stop writing now before I go on for another 3 pages. BTW: my Dad sez HI to everyone.

P.S.: Madison did u notice that today is Friday the 13th. OMG how did that happen?

Madison held her side, she was laughing so hard. It wasn't so much Lindsay's jokes, although they were funny. It was the kind of laughter that comes from deep inside: happy, secure laughter. Madison felt as though her friends were right there next to her. She could practically hear Lindsay's voice.

Madison clicked around the bigfishbowl site a little bit more; and then surfed into her e-mailbox. That was when her sentimental feelings took over.

Although Madison guessed that no one read the blog other than her friends, it was still out there in view. And she wanted to make sure that this message—her attached message—was a private one, for three sets of eyes only.

She hit NEW on Dad's computer and composed a private e-mail.

```
From: MadFinn
To: Wetwinz, LuvNstuff, BalletGrl
Subject: Walk this around pleez!!!
Date: Fri 13 Aug 10:11 PM
```
Just read everyone's blogs (three times) and I am bummed b/c ur all soooo far away. I could really use

```
u right now. In honor of my best
friends in the whole entire world,
read the attachment pleez. MYSM
. . . LYLAS . . . BFN!

((attachment :DEARFRIEND.pdf))
```

It's National Friendship Week!
Show your friends how much you care.
Send this to everyone you consider a FRIEND.
If it comes back to you,
then you'll know you have a circle of friends.
And thanks for being MY friend.

Friend: calls your parents by Mr. and Mrs.

Best friend: calls your parents Dad and Mom

Friend: laughs at your jokes when they're funny

Best friend: laughs at your jokes when they're *not* funny

Friend: borrows your stuff for a few days then gives it back

Best friend: has a closet full of your stuff

Friend: always gets you a nice birthday present

Best friend: gives you stuff even when it's *not* your birthday

Friend: only knows a few things about you

Best friend: could write a show on you for the Biography Channel

Friend: would delete this letter

**Best friend: will send this back to me and all of their online buddies--SO DO IT NOW!!!
THANKS, FRIEND!!!**

After hitting SEND, Madison turned off the computer and the light. Maybe it was the long day spent indoors or maybe it was just the rain, but something had made Madison extra tired. She stared at shadows as they danced on the walls of the apartment. There seemed to be a dancing palm tree outside Madison's window. Somehow the wind had picked up, which was strange for such a muggy, wet evening.

Madison remembered the warning that Fiona had mentioned—and that she'd seen on the Weather Channel, too. *Was* a hurricane headed for the Florida coast? The tropical depression was somewhere out in the Atlantic Ocean just then. Madison wondered if the next day she would wake up to torrential rain. Where were the tornadoes and waves and debris (and cows) flying through the air? Those were the hurricane images she knew from TV and movies.

Madison had all but given up on her loggerhead-turtle-counting trick for getting her to sleep. Tonight, she'd dream of gale-force winds instead. A hurricane dream was just the right thing to whip Madison's head and heart back into shape.

Wasn't it?

As she lay in the darkness, Madison heard voices again—coming from down the hallway. Dad and Stephanie were back at it—arguing. They seemed to be trying very hard to keep their voices down.

Madison couldn't tell what they were saying exactly, but it sounded serious. She shut her eyes tightly and tried to think of something else.

Some kind of serious stormy weather was coming. Madison knew it.

And it wasn't the kind of storm that could be helped with some stupid slicker.

Chapter 14

The weekend went by in a blur. Everyone in the county was preparing for the possibility that a hurricane might be on its way. For Madison, it seemed as if that reality had already hit. By Monday morning, her thoughts were churning. When the chirping of birds awoke her, she bounded out of bed without putting on her slippers and logged on to her computer right away.

The Parent Trap

```
Is this the Big D all over again?
I feel like Dad and Stephanie are
talking in code. I was going to write about
this in a blog or even to Bigwheels on
```

e-mail but I don't actually know where to start. They fight a lot more than I remember. Y is that? I can't tell what's normal fighting and what's bad fighting but there's this weird tension in the apartment and this was supposed to be the relaxing week coming up. Stephanie has cried at least twice since I've been here and I still don't really know why but I know it has something to do w/Dad. Aaaaargh! He just keeps telling me "Relax, Maddie. Don't sweat it."

Rude Awakening: Whenever someone says, "Relax, don't sweat it," why does it instantly feel a whole lot hotter?

Here's what happened this weekend. Saturday we went shopping in the car—the three of us. When we got to the beach town, Dad wanted to go to The Lemon Drop for lunch but Stephanie and I went there earlier this week so we told Dad we'd rather go someplace else. Well, Dad had a craving for one of The Lemon Drop's fish sandwiches and just wanted to stay there and eat on the bench and he had this little tantrum in the car—I swear. Stephanie finally talked him out of it and we went to a hamburger joint. It was this major drama for such a DUMB reason. Dad acted a little nicer after that, but I didn't feel like talking to him.

Later on after we'd eaten, we went shopping. I saw a pair of earrings—VV cool

with wooden beads and colored stones--and
Dad said I could have those if I wanted. He
didn't really care. I could tell. He was
bored. Then I saw something WAY better. I
found this pair of identical charms--and
they were alligators!! I decided that was
the better thing to buy. Maybe I can give
one to Aim or Fiona or Lindsay when we get
back to Far Hills?? Dad told me to hurry up
and pick something. He never rushes me.
What's up with that?

Sunday wasn't much better. Dad was still
acting weird so Stephanie took me to the
movies alone. The sky looked dark when we
came out and we worried that maybe the
storm was coming AGAIN, but it didn't. It
seemed like Stephanie would start confiding
in me about her and Dad, but she didn't.
Ugh!

I know I should just stay out of it.
That was my problem w/Dad and Mom, too,
when I always butted in. But it's soooo
hard not to want to help, since I heard all
their fights and all their problems too.
What am I supposed to do the second time
around? This is a question for the
Blowfish. Or for my BFFs. For anyone
but me. Sometimes I feel like maybe
this is some kind of parent trap--or
test. If I just DON'T think about it,
it'll go away.

Madison quickly hit SAVE. The clock said it was just

9:00 A.M. In a few minutes, Stephanie would be running Madison over to the ELC for Monday's rescheduled riverboat trip. There, the entire camp would board three different pontoons at precisely 10:00 A.M. and would tour on the boats through lunch. Two teams and several camp staff members were assigned to each large pontoon. Stephanie said it would be like a nature cruise; luckily, there were no gray clouds in sight.

Pontoons were good fun for groups like Madison's camp, because they were flat-bottomed boats. If the group had had to ride on a regular boat, there would have been no place to stand and move around. This way, everyone could sit or stand or shuffle around to observe the birds, fish, and, if they were really, *really* lucky, a Florida panther, one of the endangered species occasionally spotted along the coast.

Once Madison arrived at the ELC, she saw a procession of kids heading for the camp docks and the river launch. Madison wanted to say something to Stephanie about the weekend, but she didn't. Instead, she offered a regular good-bye and followed the others as they drifted down to the water. Along the way, Madison caught a glimpse of Ann and Will walking up ahead. She raced to catch up to them.

"Hey!" Madison said, a little winded from her sprint.

"Maddie!" Ann cheered.

Will gave Madison a big smile. "Mad Dog!" he said.

Madison burst into laughter. "Do you have to call me that?" She was relieved to laugh after the tension of the past few days.

Will just laughed. "Yes, I do have to call you that, Mad Dog. Why? Don't you like it, Mad Dog?"

Madison pushed Will's arm. "Stop!" she teased, even though she secretly loved the fact that he'd assigned her a special nickname.

"What's the matter, Mad Dog?" Will continued, poking her in the back.

Madison raised her arm to push Will a second time, but Ann stepped between the two of them. "Break it up, you two. I just saw one of the counselors looking over here."

Will seemed about to make some funny crack back to Ann, but just then Teeny came running up with Suchita.

"There you are!" Teeny said.

"Anyone see Logan?" Suchita asked.

The walk down to the water took a little bit longer than Madison had expected. Mangroves grew over the path in spots, and some kids (prompted by some counselors) kept stopping to identify creatures and plants along the way.

"Did you guys see Logan?" Suchita asked again.

Madison shook her head but smiled. She guessed

that Suchita had a crush on Logan. That was why she always wanted to be his partner. Madison wondered if *she* were equally transparent about her crush on Will. She hoped not. She wasn't ready for the entire universe to know about her mixed-up feelings. What if somehow Hart had found out?

"Look at *that*!" Teeny cried, pointing up at a tree. Sticking out from under a piece of bark was a long, thin snake. Its scaly skin was red, black, and yellow.

Suchita let out a little scream, and everyone jumped.

"What is *that*?"

One of the counselors rushed over.

"Stand back," she said. Then she turned to everyone with a calm look on her face. "No worries," she said. "It's a scarlet king snake."

"But I thought snakes with that many colors were bad. Isn't it poisonous?" Ann said.

The counselor shook her head. "You're thinking of the coral snake, I think. This isn't the same color combination. I know it can be confusing. Just remember this little rhyme and you'll be able to identify the snakes correctly. You look at the way the colors are lined up on a snake's body—like this: red to yellow, kills a fellow; red to black, venom lack."

"That's cool," Will said. Just as he spoke, the snake disappeared back into the tree.

Madison shuddered. She liked learning important

facts about the wildlife and reptiles—especially snakes and alligators—but it didn't make her any less scared of long, slimy, slithery things. No amount of love for animals could help Madison get over slithery things.

After more frog- and lizard-sightings, Madison and the others finally reached the water. The path opened on to a clearing where Leonard was waiting with the boatmen. The three pontoon boats were revved up and ready to go.

It didn't take long for everyone to board. The Alligators crowded in with the Flounders. The Butterflies and the Crabs were put together, too. That left the Dolphins and the Egrets. Madison, Will, Ann, and the others sat in neat rows of seats across their boat. Each boat carried about seventeen passengers in all—campers plus Camp Sunshine staffers and two other crew members.

The air felt cooler on the boat, for some reason. Madison soon realized that there was a large fan operating nearby—the driver told them that it was turned on to keep the bugs away. It had been a buggy month in the swamp. Each crew left the docks in sequence. Madison leaned forward on the edge of her seat. She'd been on boats many times before, including the time when she had been in the Amazon with Mom on one of Mom's shoots for Budge Films, and on the lake near Gramma Helen's house. But something about this trip felt different.

Maybe it was the fact that she was alone here—no parents, no grandparents.

And then there was the Will factor.

For whatever reason, this boy had gotten under Madison's skin. She kept stealing sidelong glances at him. His hair was all messy in front. He looked as if he'd just rolled out of bed. He had a tan, too, which made his skin the color of a golden raisin and made his white teeth stand out when he smiled one of his coy little smiles.

"Maddie? Is anyone in there?"

Madison shook off her daydream and realized that Leonard was standing over her.

She shot a look up at him and started to sputter. "I—I—I . . ." she said, unable to get any more words out.

"Are you okay?" Leonard repeated. "I saw you sitting here and you looked a little dizzy. Are you?"

Madison felt a hot breeze on her face. The boat was moving. She'd completely spaced out for almost a whole minute.

How embarrassing.

She glanced around and realized that while she'd been in space, Will, Teeny, Ann, and the others had moved to the side of the boat. They were looking out over the water, pointing at different things on the shore, in the water, and up in the air.

Madison swallowed hard. "I think I'm okay," she said, although she wasn't really sure.

172

Leonard smiled and offered his hand. "Why don't we join the rest of the group?" he said.

Madison stood up and shuffled over with Leonard to the crowd. There was no space near the other Egrets, so she slipped in between two Dolphins.

One of the kids who seemed about ten feet tall moved aside so Madison could see. He towered over Madison. She could hardly see his face; it was shaded by a red baseball cap.

"Hey," the boy grunted. "We just saw a blue heron."

"Oh," Madison said softly.

"Yeah, take a look," the boy said. "Over there."

He pointed, and Madison looked across the stretch of river. Along the banks, she saw a blue heron sunning itself in a glade. Brown, green, and yellow grasses grew around the area, like a carpet. The bird stood still and then moved to a rock. It appeared to turn its body and stare in Madison's direction—like a picture on a postcard.

"Look!" someone cried from the other side of the boat. Up in the sky, Madison saw what all the fuss was about. A pair of birds swooped around the tops of a tall, tall tree.

"Osprey!" Leonard announced. He gave every-one a quick tutorial about the birds and their feed-ing habits. Madison was glad to have the camp leader on her pontoon. She figured Leonard would be able to spot more wildlife on the water than anyone at the ELC.

The ospreys danced in the air. Madison had never seen anything like it; and yet she knew she must have seen ospreys before then. There was something about camp, something about this pontoon ride, that was helping Madison to see things more clearly. She was in awe of the birds' flight pattern. Their wings stretched out so they could soar higher and higher.

And then without warning, one of the ospreys dived down to the shoreline and grabbed something.

"He got lunch!" someone cried. Madison recognized Teeny's voice, and she giggled.

The osprey vanished into the trees.

The hot air smelled like fish and muck, but the occasional breeze, no matter how warm, brought some relief. Madison tilted her face back into the sunlight.

"Hey, Mad Dog! Where did you go?"

Madison blinked in the bright sunshine. Then Will's face came into focus.

He'd come looking for her?

It wasn't as if Will had had to walk far to find Madison, since there weren't many people on their boat. But he'd looked for her—and that was all that mattered to Madison.

"There wasn't enough room where you guys were standing. . . ." Madison began.

Will started to say something in reply, but then he turned around; Ann was calling to him and the rest of the Egrets.

"Will! Madison! Logan! Suchita! Teeny! Come here!"

She sounded like a drill instructor, the way she called out each of their names. But everyone raced over to see what she was fussing about. After the preceding day, of rain and rattled nerves, this was a welcome change. It felt good to be outside sharing the sky and water with the birds and fish.

During the remainder of the ride, the kids saw other birds. Leonard gave some tips on birdwatching. Madison was amazed at how much she was learning on the trip.

"Here are some tricks to identify birds. First, check out the bird's shape and its color. You should take a look at a bird's behavior, too. Is it hunting for food quickly or wading slowly through the water? Listen for its voice. You can tell a lot about a bird's temperament by its call."

"This guy knows everything," Teeny whispered to Madison.

Madison nodded, still listening.

Leonard continued. "The thing is, kids, that the ELC is located on what's called the Eastern Continental Flyway. This is a major bird-migration corridor, where shorebirds, waterfowl, raptors, and passerines stop to feed and hang out. The folks at the state bird-watching organization have identified more than three hundred different species of birds in this area alone."

Wow, Madison thought, as off in the distance a large trio of pelicans flapped by. She knew exactly what kind of birds they were. Already, she'd been able to take Leonard's tips and turn them into something.

By the time the boats pulled back in to the docks almost two hours later, most of the campers were sad to disembark. Everyone wanted a second pontoon ride. That only made Leonard laugh.

"I'm glad to see that you kids are learning something," he said. "You should get out and do your own bird-watches. Tell your friends. Do one in your own neighborhoods at home. Look up birds on the Internet."

Madison made a mental note to do so. She knew it was exactly the kind of project her friends Egg and Drew would enjoy. Anything that involved online research was right up their alley.

Along with Madison, the boys were responsible for many of Far Hills Junior High School's Web site downloads, photographs, and other site updates. Madison wondered if maybe the three of them could create links on the school site to environmental Web sites. She thought that maybe she'd speak to the science teacher, Mr. Danehy, about doing a special project. Her mind buzzed with ideas.

"Cool stuff, right?" Will said. He grinned, and Madison felt herself grin right back. The grin was contagious. They were on the same wavelength, there was no better feeling.

The Egrets walked back to the ELC together. Madison realized that she'd been so consumed by the fun on the pontoon boat that she had worried less about Ann that day. Ann seemed just as excited by the day's events, and hadn't talked as much as she usually did.

Sometimes, Madison thought, there were things that were bigger than the six of them. Sometimes it was better just to hang back and let things fly (literally) overhead before sinking in.

Lunch and the rest of the afternoon weren't nearly as exciting as the morning boat trip, but Madison didn't mind. By the time Stephanie and Dad came (together) to pick her up in front of the ELC at the end of the day, she was still beaming.

The ride back to the apartment was strangely quiet. Dad and Stephanie didn't argue as they had the day before. But something was still stuck in the air between them.

Madison started to tell them about the ospreys and the king snake with its red skin. But for some reason, neither Dad nor Stephanie were listening as closely as they usually did.

So Madison stopped talking. She stared out the window. When she got back to the apartment,

Madison thought, she would Insta-Message one of her BFFs. Aimee would "get it." Or maybe Fiona would.

The apartment was icy cool. Madison stepped inside and realized just how hot it had been out there on the boat all morning. She decided to take a shower and then check her e-mailbox. She would do that and then blog.

Meanwhile, Dad and Stephanie remained as silent as before. Dad mentioned that he was planning to grill some marinated chicken fillets for dinner. Stephanie was making a tossed salad and steamed broccoli. They said nothing more, and Madison didn't push it. She figured that after her experiences poking her nose into Dad and Stephanie's fights, it was better to stay out of it. A hands-off approach was the right one for Madison, Dad, and Stephanie.

After a quick shower, Madison slathered herself in some cucumber-melon lotion that Mom had given her for the trip. It smelled very fresh. Madison's skin was flushed from the sun, but the cream cooled her down.

She dressed in a pair of sweat shorts and a pink T-shirt. Then Madison sat down at her laptop and logged onto bigfishbowl.com. There were no e-mails in her e-mailbox.

Hart had not written.

He'd said he'd E Madison, but she knew he might not. It was a big step—to E each other long distance.

They'd only just recently admitted their feelings of like.

Madison clicked NEW and decided that she would send *him* an e-mail. She began to type in the subject line.

Subject: Miss You!

Then Madison promptly deleted what she'd typed. That was *way* too much. She retyped.

Subject: Where R U?

No, Madison told herself. That sounded too desperate. She adjusted the subject line one last time, as generically as she could possibly get it without sounding too aloof. It had to be just right or she'd give Hart the wrong message—and that could be disastrous.

From: MadFinn
To: Sk8ingboy
Subject: Hello There
Date: Mon 16 Aug 5:34 PM
So I've been waiting for a letter
from you. Remember we said we'd
write? I know I could have e-mailed
u b4 now but it's been way busy
here @ camp. How about you?

DELETE. DELETE. DELETE.

Madison typed and retyped her message but then discarded the note altogether.

She couldn't send Hart an e-mail. Not like this.

She surfed around the site a little bit more. At one point, Madison's Insta-Message key went *ding*. Surprise! Fiona was logged on, too. How lucky, Madison thought, as she sent Fiona her first Florida-based Insta-Message. The pair decided upon a private "room" where they could go to chat live.

```
<MadFinn>: so howz Los Gatos??
<Wetwinz>: OK how's Florida
<MadFinn>: OK camp is so great
    Fiona u'd love it ALL esp.
    today we went on this boat
    trip. PONTOON (cool word
    right?)
<Wetwinz>: I like all kinds of
    boats
<MadFinn>: so . . . weren't u
    supposed 2 see Julio 2day or
    yesterday?
<Wetwinz>: yes
<MadFinn>: well how did it go???
<Wetwinz>: IDW2T@I
<MadFinn>: You were blabbing
    about him B4. what happened??
<Wetwinz>: well we saw each other
    that's true
```

Madison waited for Fiona to type in more information. But two minutes later, Fiona still had written
nothing more.

```
<MadFinn>: R U THERE?
<Wetwinz>: Maddie I can't tell u
   what happened
<MadFinn>: Since when???
<Wetwinz>: it's not good
<MadFinn>: OMG what happened?
<Wetwinz>: Maddie u have 2 promise
   u won't be mad @ me
<MadFinn>: What's the matter
<Wetwinz>: PROMISE
<MadFinn>: ok ok I promise
<Wetwinz>: Julio kissed me just like
   last year
```

Madison nearly fell off her chair when she read
Fiona's text.

```
<MadFinn>: RYKM????
<Wetwinz>: pleez don't be mad @ me
<MadFinn>: what about Egg? OMG Fiona
   Egg would DIE if he knew
<Wetwinz>: I know. he can't know.
<MadFinn>: F?
<Wetwinz>: pleez Maddie I know what
   ur thinking
<MadFinn>: so what now? do u like
   Julio again?
```

\<Wetwinz\>: NO it was so awful and I told him not to do it and he was embarrassed. It was SO WEIRD

\<MadFinn\>: r u ok?

\<Wetwinz\>: I miss Egg.

\<MadFinn\>: um . . . does Chet know?

\<Wetwinz\>: NO WAY & u can't tell n e one not even Lindsay b/c she likes to gossip sometimes and Aimee 2. I'm trusting u 2 keep this secret PLEEZ u have 2 keep this a secret--take it to your grave

\<MadFinn\>: I will. Don't worry I will

\<Wetwinz\>: I don't know what I was thinking but I missed all my friends here so much and Julio was soooo nice it was like it was b4 I left and then w/Dad talking about moving back. I let Julio kiss me. I know I did. Some teeny part of me must have wanted to.

\<MadFinn\>: I thought u said that wuz just talk about you & him.

\<Wetwinz\>: Just talk? Dad and Mom sound pretty serious. Dad even called someone about shifting his job back again

\<MadFinn\>: OMG RUKM?

\<Wetwinz\>: don't worry it'll work

out
<MadFinn>: yeah and you'll be there
    & not here FIONA U CAN'T GO BACK
    THERE
<Wetwinz>: I know but I don't have
    a choice it's up to Mom & Dad

Madison stopped typing and shook out her fingers. What was this? Fiona was writing all these things that Madison just did not want to read.

Moving to Los Gatos again? Leaving Far Hills?

When Fiona had talked about such things the week before it had seemed unlikely, but now, it seemed as if Madison's worst fear might come true.

Would Fiona really be moving away?

They could hardly be BFFs across an entire country. Madison's heart felt heavy. She had wanted to share many things with Fiona about the past week: the Egrets and the faraway look in Will's green eyes and the way the water shimmered under the super-hot Florida sun. But she couldn't bring herself to tell Fiona anything about any of that.

She could hardly bring herself to write a single word.

Chapter 15

The beach on Tuesday was steamy hot, just as Monday had been.

Since the heat and high humidity were not going anywhere, Leonard and the camp staff organized an afternoon trip across one of the ponds, along a path, and across the main road toward the ocean. The ELC maintained about 500 yards of oceanfront. There was a breeze blowing off the water.

The campers were thrilled to see the nesting sites of the loggerhead turtles for the first time. Each site was marked and identified as a nest by county officials, who had placed little orange flags on wooden sticks in the sand to show where the nesting areas were.

Leonard explained to everyone about the Habitat

Conservation Plan, an agreement to limit the building of seawalls in coastal Florida.

"Everywhere you go in Florida," Leonard sighed, "you have to watch out for the natural boundaries established by the turtles. We can't just come in and wreak havoc on the beach. This is an important law meant to protect turtles from people like us."

"Whoa," Will muttered. "Who would want to hurt a turtle?"

"My dad volunteers for that group, the conservation group," Teeny said. "There are a lot of people who live here who care what happens to the water and the beach and rivers."

"That's so great," Madison said, impressed.

After a few more words from Leonard, the kids spread out across the beach. The different groups intermingled as they checked out the turtle nesting sites. Sometimes the nesting site was a deep hole; at other times, it was just a pile of sand where the turtle had been.

The campers seemed happy to check out the beach. Of course, they were also psyched to slather on a little sunblock and hang out—even just for a little while.

Unfortunately, Madison wasn't psyched—not at all. And after a half hour or so on the beach, she began to experience some real discomfort. Madison realized that she should have brought a hat; her skin was starting to prickle. She could see her arm from the shoulder to the elbow turning pink right before her very eyes—and it wasn't pretty.

Madison looked for someone to commiserate with, but she didn't find one among the Egrets. The boys could not have cared less. As for the girls, Suchita's skin appeared super tanned already, and Ann didn't have to worry about the sun, she bragged, because not only had she brought along some sunblock but her skin never, ever burned anyway. As much as Madison hated being pale, even worse was being *alone* in her paleness.

Lindsay and Aimee would have related to paleness. They could all have hidden from the sun together. At that exact moment, Madison missed her BFFs more than ever.

Thankfully, the ongoing hunt for turtle nests and other beach artifacts made Madison forget all about the tanning dilemma. With Ann and Suchita she teamed up to make notes about their beach observations, while the boys teamed up to take their own notes. Madison was momentarily wistful about not being paired with Will in any way (at least for a little while), but she didn't dwell on it. Hanging with the girls was an opportunity for better bonding with them. It was like having temporary substitutes for Aimee and Fiona—almost.

Leonard and his staff strolled around. They asked the campers to look for shells, to identify insects, and to seek out the small holes where crabs hid. They wanted everyone to pay attention to the things on the beach, from seashells to seaweed. The campers needed to learn all they could about that habitat so that they could knowledgeably observe the turtles laying their eggs during hatchling night.

The big event was only a few days away. It was the defining moment of Camp Sunshine. In just a few nights, all of the campers—from Alligators to Flounders—would band together on that very beach to observe the loggerhead turtles in the darkness as they crawled up the beach to lay their eggs. Of course, there was the chance that there might not be many turtles on the beach that particular night; but there was also a chance that there would be dozens of them.

Madison had her fingers crossed. She wanted to see as many turtles as possible. She had a vision of a beach filled with so many turtles that there was no sand visible, nowhere to walk: a blanket of turtles creeping up from the ocean's edge.

Now, that would be cool.

Ann found a large piece of driftwood shaped like antlers, and after singing a rousing "only-126-days-until-Christmas" chorus of "Rudolph the Red-Nosed Reindeer," she buried the wood in the sand.

Madison laughed. "That was funny," she said. With all of Ann's quirks, had Madison simply missed her sense of humor? Maybe Ann wasn't so annoying after all. Maybe she was just trying hard to get everyone to like her.

That was a feeling Madison understood only too well.

Suchita continued her search for a bottle or some shards of beach glass. She wanted her own meaningful souvenir of this place and these people. Madison told Ann and Suchita about the note in a bottle that Madison had found the week before. Everyone agreed that finding a mysterious note in a bottle had to be good luck, somehow.

Madison wondered what the good luck would bring. Did it mean that she and Will would continue to make some kind of connection?

Then she chased that idea right out of her head.

What was she thinking? What about Hart?

Just then, the boys from the Egrets came over to the three Egret girls. The boys' hands were filled with shells of all colors, including beige, lavender, coral, and gray.

"Ooooh," Ann gushed. "Where did you find all those?"

Logan snickered. "We've been doing our homework. Where have you been?"

"Very funny," Suchita said, giggling. "We've been working, too." She held up a handful of beach glass. There was one beautiful blue shard right on top. Logan took it in his hand for a closer look.

"So, Will," Ann asked, "where did you and Teeny go?"

Madison didn't say anything.

Will grinned. "We went surfing," he cracked. "Where do you think, Ann? We were scoping out the nests."

"So were we," Madison said.

Ann smiled. "Yeah, so were we."

"Anyway," Teeny said. "Leonard just told us that they're ready to head back. You want to walk back with us?"

Will came closer to where Madison and Ann stood.

"You want to walk back together?" he asked, repeating Teeny's invitation. Madison wasn't sure to whom he was directing his question.

"Yes," Ann responded right away.

"Most excellent," Will said. He held out his hand. "So this is for you."

Once again, Madison didn't know who the *you* referred to. Ann stared at Will's open palm and snatched a beautiful pink shell that was resting in it.

"It's so pretty!" Ann said as she cradled the shell.

"Yeah, we found this depression in the sand over there with all these incredible shells. Hardly any of them are chipped. There were a lot of clamshells, too, with deep purple ridges. Very cool," Will said.

"Oh," Madison said. "I'll have to look for it."

"Yeah," Will said. "So, you want one, too?"

189

Madison reached out and took a pink shell for herself. Will smiled when she clutched it in her fingers.

"Thanks," Madison said.

"Yeah, thanks," Ann said, her eyes open wide, lashes flickering.

They started the long walk back to the ELC.

"What happened to you?" Dad asked as he drove Madison home that afternoon. He said he'd run home early from his work meeting so he could meet her.

"What do you mean, 'What happened'?" Madison asked dumbly.

"Maddie, dear, you look like a lobster," Dad said. "Does it hurt?"

Madison panicked. She pulled down the little mirror on the passenger-seat visor.

Her skin was bright pink. She was more sunburned than she'd ever been, at least since she had been a little girl. Madison remembered a time in first grade when she had gone on a trip to Chicago with Mom and Dad. She'd stayed in the lake up by Gramma Helen's house all day long without using sunscreen. That sunburn had sent her to the emergency room.

This burn wasn't nearly as bad, but it did hurt. Madison felt a little case of the chills coming on, but she wasn't sure if maybe part of that was due to the transition from hot beach to air-conditioned car.

Dad was acting very affectionate. He didn't seem as preoccupied with work as he'd been before. Instead, he seemed eager to talk about Madison's day. Of course, she obliged. She told him about the turtle nests and the pink shells. She told him about how nice Ann and Suchita had been, and about the many new friends she'd found at camp after only a week.

Dad beamed. "I knew it was a good idea, your coming down to Florida," he said. "Say, I thought we might play a game of tennis tonight. Are you up for it?"

Madison's skin was so hot to the touch. What if she got clipped by a tennis ball on top of that?

"Um . . . I don't think so, Dad," Madison said. "Can we do it another time this week?"

"Of course, sweetheart," Dad said gently, reaching out for Madison's hand. His skin was cool on top of hers. "I understand," he said.

Madison looked down at Dad's hand. She thought back to the night before she had left Far Hills, when Hart had taken her hand into his and squeezed hard. It was such a big step. She couldn't believe that he'd taken it.

"What are you grinning about?" Dad asked.

Madison quickly wiped the grin off her face. "Nothing," she lied. "I was just thinking about how happy I am to be here with you and Stephanie. That's all. Really."

"Okay," Dad said. "I believe you."

They pulled into the driveway of the apartment complex, and Dad rolled up the car windows.

"Still looks like it might rain some more," he said. "They claim this hurricane is just offshore. It's stalled. Most of the weathermen say it's headed north, but I don't know what to think. This is a stormy time of year down here. You can never be too sure of anything—especially the weather."

When they went upstairs to the apartment, Madison clicked on the Weather Channel. She wanted to hear all the hurricane talk for herself.

The woman standing in front of the meteorological map had to have been eight months pregnant. She pointed north and then south. The camera zoomed in on the map for a closer look at Florida. Then the screen changed. They put up a color map of the storm systems out in the Atlantic. Madison saw a blur of red, yellow, and green in the water. It was moving, shaping itself into a spinning circle.

"Wow," Dad said, walking into the room. "Stephanie, come look at this!"

Stephanie came in, too. The three of them sat together in front of the television, transfixed. Apparently, the stalled storm was on the move again—and it was headed directly for the central coast of Florida.

"There's still a big chance this storm will shift to the north," the weather woman said, speaking

192

directly to the camera, "but folks along the coast from Vero Beach to Cape Canaveral should expect to see some heavy wind and rain—or worse. Tune in for another update at twenty minutes past the hour."

Madison sighed. "A hurricane is really going to hit?" she cried. "But it can't."

"I know it seems unbelievable." Dad shook his head. "The coast is really getting battered these days. At least everyone's serious about the danger now."

"Yeah," Madison exclaimed. "But I'm serious about some other stuff, too. Like, what happens to camp and hatchling night if there's a hurricane? What happens to the turtles? What happens to—"

Madison wanted to say, "Will," but she stopped herself.

"I never thought about the hatchlings," Stephanie said. "If there are heavy tides, those poor turtles lose their eggs and nests, don't they?"

Madison was overwhelmed by the thought. "Yes," she said. Her voice sank to barely a whisper. "What happens then?"

Dad clicked off the TV and suggested the three of them have dinner and change the subject. Stephanie had made macaroni and cheese, one of her specialties, and a huge tossed salad. Everyone pulled up to the dinner table.

At the start of the meal, the three of them sat in silence, their forks clanking against the plates. Dad sipped his glass of wine and chewed his food loudly.

Stephanie didn't say much. She picked at her salad. "Jeff," she said.

Madison looked up when she heard Stephanie's voice.

"What?" Dad asked. His voice sounded distant, not the way it had in the car.

"So I went to the doctor today," Stephanie said.

Dad shot Stephanie a look.

"I know that," he said. His mood seemed to shift suddenly from neutral to angry.

"So . . ." Stephanie said.

Dad dropped his utensils onto his plate. "Steph—I thought we agreed we would not say anything—"

"Jeff, I just think we should tell Madison."

Madison's ears pricked up for sure.

Tell me what?

"No!" Dad's voice boomed. He stood up from the table. "Absolutely not. I can't believe you would shanghai me like this—in front of her—"

"You mean *me*?" Madison said.

"You keep out of this!" Dad cried.

Madison sank down in her seat, a forkful of macaroni and cheese still in her hand. Dad had never raised his voice like that at her.

"I'm sorry," Stephanie started to say.

"I'm—I'm—" Dad didn't know what else to say. He grabbed his wineglass and disappeared into his office. He didn't even look back.

The table fell silent. Stephanie's breathing was deep, very deep.

Then, all at once, she began to cry again.

Madison was freaking out. She'd never heard Dad and Stephanie fight, and now they seemed to end each day with some kind of explosion—and this was the worst *ever*. How could Dad have gone from kind to crazy-mad in just a few minutes? What was on his mind? What was going on? What didn't he want Madison to know?

Stephanie wasn't saying. She got up from the table, barely having touched her food, and walked toward her bedroom. On the way, however, she caressed the top of Madison's shoulder.

"I'm so sorry, Maddie," Stephanie said. "We have lousy timing, your dad and I—well, we're just in the middle of something—and I can't really explain. It really has nothing to do with you. Well, I just wanted to . . . You should ask him about it. Okay?"

"But—" Madison blurted out. Many questions were flying into her head.

But no answers.

Stephanie walked away, shutting the door behind her. Madison looked around the room. She was shaking. Was it because of what had happened between Dad and Stephanie—or was it just the sunburn?

Madison couldn't be sure. In the silence of the dining room, she didn't know what else to do, so she continued to eat her macaroni. At least she was hungry. The day on the beach had worked up her appetite in spite of the sunburn—and the bad vibes.

As she sat at the table by herself, Madison noticed a square package sitting across the room. She recognized the shape. Jumping down off her chair, Madison raced over to unwrap the brown paper that covered the object.

My laptop! Dad had it fixed!

Madison tore away the paper and gave her precious laptop the once-over. Then, as both Dad and Stephanie had done, she retreated into her room and shut the door.

With both of them having taken to their separate corners of the apartment, and Madison still unsure about which one to talk to, there remained only one thing for her to do: write in her files.

Madison logged on to bigfishbowl.com to post a new blog entry. But then she changed her mind. She was having private thoughts—not public ones. Even though a blog would probably be seen only by her BFFs, Madison wasn't sure she could share these thoughts even with them.

Instead of blogging, Madison opened a file.

 Getting Burned

Rude Awakening: Just when I think my life is in the pink (literally--I am covered in sunburn!), something happens to wash me right out again.

So I've been butting out of all this Dad and Stephanie stuff. But now it seems worse than ever and I am really REALLY worried. I thought about calling Mom to ask her about it but THAT would be pretty stupid, right? I mean, she doesn't exactly care about Dad's love life now, does she? She's too busy dating her own lineup of weirdos LOL.

I keep thinking about what Fiona and I were talking about the other night online. I was being so harsh to her about Julio. But meanwhile, I'm practically doing the same thing with Hart and Will, right? Why do people have secrets? We all do, I guess. Dad and Stephanie seem to have a HUGE one they won't tell me about.

Rude Awakening: Sometimes the hurricane brewing inside seems way worse than the hurricane brewing outside.

Which one will hit first?

19341 TCARTF-GO
EMERGENCY BULLETIN

TROPICAL DEPRESSION THIRTEEN INTERMEDIATE ADVISORY NUMBER 1A NWS TPC/NATIONAL HURRICANE CENTER MIAMI FL

2 AM EST TUES AUG 17

TROPICAL STORM WARNING REMAINS IN EFFECT
FOR THE TURKS AND CAICOS . . . TROPICAL STORM
WARNING MEANS THAT TROPICAL STORM
CONDITIONS ARE EXPECTED WITHIN THE
WARNING AREA WITHIN THE NEXT 24 HOURS.

HURRICANE WATCH REMAINS IN EFFECT FOR THE
NORTHWEST BAHAMAS. HURRICANE WATCH
MEANS THAT HURRICANE CONDITIONS ARE
POSSIBLE WITHIN THE WATCH AREA . . .
GENERALLY WITHIN 36 HOURS.

INTERESTS IN SOUTH FLORIDA AND THE FLORIDA
KEYS . . . AND IN CENTRAL AND WESTERN CUBA
SHOULD CLOSELY MONITOR THE PROGRESS OF THIS
SYSTEM OVER THE NEXT FEW DAYS.

ESTIMATED MIN. CENTRAL PRESSURE IS 1009
MB . . . 29.80 INCHES. THE DEPRESSION IS EXPECTED
TO PRODUCE TOTAL RAIN ACCUMULATIONS OF 3
TO 5 INCHES OVER MUCH OF THE ABOVE AREAS
WITH POSSIBLE ISOLATED RAINFALL OF 8 INCHES.

NEXT ADVISORY WILL BE ISSUED BY THE NATIONAL
HURRICANE CENTER (NHC) AT 5 AM EST.

FORECASTER DI CARLO

Chapter 16

After the big (and weird) Dad-Stephanie conflict on Tuesday night, Madison found herself preoccupied with thoughts of an inevitable breakup between her dad and her stepmother. Her only point of reference was the separation between Dad and her own mom, and for them, all the disagreement and fighting had led to one place: divorce court.

Why should this be any different?

Although Wednesday afternoon at camp was enjoyable, Madison felt a little as though she weren't really there. She couldn't stop thinking about Dad and Stephanie, naturally. She also thought about the very long hurricane bulletin she'd downloaded from the Internet the night before—the document full of storm warnings. It had been a jumble of coordinates and directions, and was beginning to worry Madison more than she'd realized.

Everyone split into their groups to prepare for hatchling night on Thursday. Kids readied their little notebooks, made lists of supplies, and plotted the nesting areas they would stake out for observation. Since she wasn't feeling well, Madison let Ann do all the talking for the Egrets. Will and the other boys spent most of the day cracking jokes among themselves, but Madison didn't really feel like joking around. But when, after an intense week and a half together, Suchita and Ann started to get all mushy about camp, Madison joined in.

"I know we've only been here for a week," Suchita declared in the middle of lunch that day. "But I feel like I've known both of you for longer."

"That is *so* true," Ann declared. "We're like beach sisters."

Madison laughed out loud. Ann was right.

"Do you guys have best friends back home?" Madison asked, thinking of her own BFFs.

Suchita nodded fiercely. "Oh, yeah," she said. "Me and my cousin Raya are best, *best* pals."

"Not me," Ann said. "At the end of school this year, I sort of broke up with my friends."

"What?" Madison turned to her. "What do you mean, you broke up with them? Why would you break up with a friend?"

"You just do," Ann said. "My friend Patti said I

200

was a geek. She said she'd rather hang out with the cooler kids. I don't know what changed. I don't think I changed. It really bummed me out."

"Wow," Suchita said. "That *is* a bummer."

"*Your friend* changed," Madison declared. She thought about herself and Poison Ivy. "A while back, my best friend turned into my best enemy," she said. "And she's still the enemy."

"Wow," Suchita said again, louder this time. "I've never had any enemies. Not really. You guys are way ahead of me in the friend thing."

"The truth is, my friend Patti isn't really my enemy," Ann said. "I don't want her to be. The truth is, I just want her friendship back again. You know?"

Madison smiled knowingly. "I know," she said softly.

Something about the exchange with Madison's new friends made her feel better about all the rough feelings she'd been having the previous night and that morning.

At the end of the day, Will made a point of coming over to Madison when she was standing by herself. He looked nervous. She wasn't sure why, but he made her feel nervous, too.

"So . . . will I see you later?" he asked quietly.

"Why are you whispering?" Madison asked, just as quietly.

Will coughed. "I'm not," he said. "I just asked a question. Um . . ."

201

Madison crossed her arms in front of her. "You mean tomorrow, right?"

"Yeah," Will said. Then he shook his head. "Actually, I was wondering if maybe you wanted to come with me—well, me and my grandpa Ralph, tonight. I mean, your whole family should come, too, obviously. Riverside Mini-Golf has this special on Wednesday nights. And I asked some of the other camp kids to come, too. That's what I wanted to ask."

"You want to play mini-golf? With me?" Madison was floored by the invite. "Tonight? I have to ask. But . . . I think it'll be okay."

"Okay? Okay. That's cool," Will said. "You have the phone contact list, right? So you can call me when you get home."

"Right, home," Madison said. She didn't know what else to say.

"Okay, then . . ." Will said. "Okay, then."

As he walked away, Madison said, "Who else is coming?"

But he had already gone.

Ann came over just afterward with a curious look on her face.

"What's up?" she asked Madison.

"My temperature," Madison joked. "I still feel kind of woozy from this sunburn. Ha-ha."

Ann laughed. "No-o-o-o! I meant what was Will asking you?"

"Will?" Madison wanted to tell Ann, but she

202

didn't. Something made her keep Will's invitation a secret.

"I didn't say anything before now, but Will is so cute, right?" Ann said with a wide smile. There was a long pause. Her eyes were still locked on the space Will had occupied. "Don't you think so?"

Madison nodded. "Uh-huh."

"Can I tell you a secret?" Ann asked. "I think maybe Will likes me—just a little."

"Yeah," Madison said with a sigh.

Ann leaned over and gave Madison one of the hanging-on hugs. Madison tried pulling back, but the grip was tighter than tight. A moment later, Ann turned on her heel and bounded toward the front door of the ELC. "See you tomorrow," she called back to Madison and Suchita. "I am so psyched for the big day."

Madison didn't know what to think—or say— after Ann left. She wasn't used to being the one in this position when it came to liking boys. She was used to being the one who *didn't* get asked to go out—not the one who *did*.

Once out the door, Madison made a beeline for the parking lot to search for Dad and Stephanie's car.

She wondered how the rest of the night would turn out.

"Let's motor, Maddie!" Stephanie called out. "Clock's ticking!"

"Yeah, Maddie," Dad grumbled. He wasn't happy about having to go play miniature golf, but Stephanie had twisted his arm.

"I don't know what to wear!" Madison cried. "I just—have to—finish getting—dressed—"

Madison was stuck as to which pants to wear. Would it be jeans pair number one (boot cut, faded, button fly), or jeans pair number two (the ones that never felt like jeans but rather like stretchy leggings)? Then she held up a flowered skirt instead and pulled that on. It would be cooler, and anyway it matched her strappy red sandals. . . .

What am I doing?

Madison sat down on the bed for a moment more. She thought about Hart, back home in Far Hills. What would he have said if he had known that she was heading out to play mini-golf with another boy? And what would Ann say tomorrow when she found out? Was Madison overthinking this—as she overthought *everything*?

"Maddie," Stephanie said softly from the doorway to Madison's room. "I really think we'd better go before Dad changes his mind."

Madison smiled. "Okay. I'm coming."

There were many reasons Dad didn't want to go. For starters, he wasn't sure he liked the idea of Madison hanging out with a boy she'd only just met.

"This isn't actually a *date*, is it?" Dad asked as they got into the car.

"Of course not," Madison said. "Dad, I'm only twelve. I don't date, remember? Besides, I can't date Will anyway. I like someone else. And someone else likes Will, too, so . . ."

Stephanie chuckled at Madison's babbling, but Dad set his jaw and scowled.

"*Whom* do you like?" Dad asked.

Madison looked down at the upholstery of the car so she wouldn't have to meet Dad's eyes in the rearview mirror.

"I like Hart. Back home, Dad. Remember? You've met him a few times."

"Oh, Hart. Yes," Dad said, although Madison was pretty sure he didn't remember a thing about him.

Stephanie gazed silently out the window. Madison tried talking to her once or twice, but all she got was a nod or a shrug. Things between Stephanie and Dad still felt funny.

When they got stuck in traffic off Main Street, where all the fast-food restaurants and attractions were located, Dad turned on the radio. A classical station came on. Stephanie quickly changed the station to soft rock. A slow song came on that Madison didn't recognize. Dad and Stephanie knew it, though. They mouthed the words. Madison could tell, even from all the way in the backseat. She was watching their every move.

Somewhere in the middle of the song, Stephanie let out a little gasp, and then Dad made a funny,

205

angry face and then—wait!—was Stephanie crying? Dad reached over for a squeeze of Stephanie's knee, but instead of taking his hand as she normally did, Stephanie pushed it away.

"Look!" Stephanie said. "We're here."

Madison looked, too. In front of the car was an enormous neon sign: RIVERSIDE MINI-GOLF.

The parking lot was *packed*.

Stephanie got out of the car with Madison while Dad went to find a space in the lot next door. Madison wanted to ask Stephanie if something—anything—was wrong, but she held her tongue. Stephanie would talk if she wanted to. It was obvious she didn't want to.

Madison's eyes scanned the crowds. Dozens of people waited on benches that lined the sides of a long sidewalk, waiting for their rounds of mini-golf to begin. Madison spotted Will, waving his arms like a windmill.

"There he is!" Madison said, cocking her head in his direction. "Up at the front of the line."

Stephanie grinned. "I see."

Will's usually shaggy hair was combed back nicely. In one hand he carried a chocolate-and-vanilla-swirl cone from the Mr. Frostee ice cream truck parked near the mini-golf entrance. In the other hand he held a mini–golf club with a blue-taped shaft. His grandparents were with him.

"So," Will's grandfather said, greeting Madison and Stephanie as they approached, "we have been waiting for this all day—a chance to meet Will's newest camp friend. Madeleine, is it?"

"It's Madison, Pops," Will told his grandfather.

Madison chuckled. Stephanie extended her hand to both of Will's grandparents.

"Hello, I'm Madison's stepmother. Madison's dad is parking the car," she said quietly.

"Well, howdy-do," Grandpa Ralph said.

"Let me go get our clubs," Stephanie said, excusing herself.

Madison nodded. Then she glanced around for other kids from camp. Was Ann lurking nearby? Had Suchita or Logan come to play?

"Um . . . where is everyone else?" Madison asked.

"Uh . . . Teeny's on the way." Will smiled, taking an enormous bite of his ice-cream cone. Half of it ended up on the ground, but Madison pretended not to notice. "And?" Madison asked.

"And . . . that's it."

"That's it?" Madison said. Only one other person from camp would be there? And it was a boy—not another girl? She felt strangely thrilled by the prospect of this and tried to hide the excitement in her voice. Maybe Dad wasn't so wrong after all. *Was* this a date?

It was at least a half date, Madison thought—if such things as half dates existed. She was, of course, overthinking the whole thing again.

Just breathe. Breathe.

The entire mini-golf complex soaked up the white-and-blue glow from the large lights in the parking lot. The eighteen–hole golf course was full of oddly shaped structures and signs. One sign bragged how the golf course was world-renowned because of its funnily themed holes. Another sign read: ENTER AT YOUR OWN RISK with a smaller line at the bottom that said, YOU MAY DIE LAUGHING.

Madison felt her pulse rate increase just standing there. The word popped into her head once again. But this wasn't a date, was it?

A moment later, Stephanie dragged over their three clubs, some colored golf balls, and a large soda. Then Dad arrived with a big smile on his face, car keys jangling in one hand, and the opposite hand extended in greeting.

"Glad to meet you, too, Jeff," Grandpa Ralph said warmly. After a second round of introductions and chatter, a cell phone went off.

Dad felt in the pockets of his linen jacket for his phone. Stephanie quickly checked her own purse. Then Will reached inside his pocket.

"Yo, hey," Will said as he flipped open his phone. "We're here, waiting. We're almost to the front of the line. Where are you?"

Madison tried not to stare while Will talked.
Will had his own cell phone?
He got off after a minute.

"That was Teeny," Will said. "His mom is coming

to drive him over here right now. She had to work today, so they're running a little bit late. . . ."

"Oh." Madison remembered that Teeny was one of the campers who actually lived in Florida year-round. If they didn't make it in time for the first tee off, Teeny and his mom could catch up with everyone after a hole or two.

At last, Madison, Will, Ralph, Dad, and Stephanie found themselves at the front of the mini-golf line. A sculpture of a purple hippo was there to greet them; a tape recorder inside the statue played an Elvis song. The whole scene was straight out of someone's crazy mind. Madison loved it.

Will placed his green golf ball on the first rubber tee mat.

"You swing," he said to Madison, leaning over to bow like a prince bowing to a princess in a movie. Madison gave it a try, but her wide swing hardly moved the ball. A divot the size of Madison's fist now rested on the mat.

Giggling, Madison did her best to hit the golf ball (and not the divot) toward the hole.

Will hit his ball next. It rolled up the steep incline toward a lighthouse that sat up on a miniature bluff, but then rolled back down again. This was a tough hole. Stephanie, Dad, and Grandpa Ralph, in that order, hit balls after that. In order to get to the hole, each golfer needed to hit the ball into one of three bigger holes at the bottom of the base of the lighthouse. Madison missed all three holes at least four times and watched as the ball rolled right back down to her. After a few tries, she was up to a 14 on a par four hole.

Mega-embarrassing.

The second hole was a teeny-weeny bit better. This hole brought Madison face-to-face with an enormous pirate ship. At least it was a big target—or so she thought. Madison aimed her club straight at the boat so she wouldn't risk blowing the shot.

POP.

Madison's ball rolled harder than ever, right into a hole on the right side of the ship.

Will laughed. He seemed to know what would happen next. He'd been playing this mini-golf course every summer since he was nine.

"The ball will come out," Will warned. "But it will get stuck somewhere in the corner, and you will definitely have wasted two shots on this one—unless the ship moves. Sometimes it does that."

Madison watched with joy as the ship lifted up and shifted to the side just as Will had said it might. And like magic, her ball drifted into the right hole.

"Congratulations, Maddie," Stephanie cheered from behind them. "How did you do that?"

Madison smiled at Will. "I don't know," she said coyly.

Dad gave Madison a round of applause, which embarrassed her.

As the group finished up on the second hole and headed over to the third, Teeny finally showed up. His mother was dressed in a dress and high heels.

"I should have changed my clothes!" Teeny's mom declared as soon as they walked up. She was definitely overdressed for mini-golf.

Then again, so was Madison, in her flowered skirt.

"Maddie! You're here," Teeny said, sounding surprised when he saw her standing there. "Where are Logan and the others?" he asked.

"They couldn't make it," Will said.

"Did you ask Suchita and Ann?" Madison asked.

Will shrugged. "Yeah. 'Course."

"So they're coming?" Teeny asked, sounding even more surprised.

"Nah," Will said. "Maddie's the only girl."

Madison realized that she was the only one who had been invited for the night. Although it felt awkward to be the only girl, there was another part of her, deep inside, that was thrilled to be the center of the boys' attention. She'd never had that happen before—not like this.

The next few mini-golf shots were even better. The third hole required a straight shot at a bucking bronco with a cowboy on its back. The fourth hole had a sequence of large bumps on an imaginary racetrack for cars. And the fifth hole, unlike the others, was mostly underground. Madison could see the ball traveling through a series of Lucite tunnels. She managed to get a par four on that hole—one stroke better than either Will *or* Teeny.

Dad and Stephanie stayed behind Madison, Teeny, and Will, but Madison turned around at one point and saw them laughing together. Teeny's mom and Will's grandparents were laughing, too.

"You know, your dad and mom are really nice," Will said.

"No doubt," Teeny said.

"Except that's not my mom," Madison said quickly. "She's my stepmom."

"Oh. Sorry," Will corrected himself. "*Stepmom.*"

"What? Does she make you clean out fireplaces, like Cinderella?" Teeny asked playfully.

"Yeah," Will joked. "Where are your wicked stepsisters?"

Madison faked an over-the-top laugh. "Ha-ha-ha! Wanna see my crystal slipper?"

Will and Teeny laughed and then took off for the sixth hole, leaving Madison a few steps behind. Madison tried not to let their swift departure bother her. She focused on the game again as best she could. She teamed up with Dad and Stephanie for a few holes.

Hole six had a water hazard: a pond behind a large turtle. Madison wondered what would happen if all the loggerhead turtles were to head there instead of to the beach. She aced the hole. The remaining nine holes got Madison's nerves frazzled, but she tried her best to appear calm and knowledgeable. After all, this was only miniature golf.

The remainder of the mini-golf evening turned into a bit of a blur. The adults (following not so closely behind) seemed to be having as good a time as the kids. Dad was a big hit, telling a whole catalog of his bad jokes.

"What's a good place to take golf clubs after hours?" Dad asked, and then quickly slapped his knee (really, his *knee*) and said, "A tee party! Get it?"

Grandpa Ralph thought that was just hysterical.

Madison tried to pretend she didn't know any of them. She raced along to catch up with the boys.

One by one, the three campers conquered other obstacles along the course, from the Statue of Liberty replica to the super coaster with 700 actual wooden pieces and a five–foot ball drop. There was a rocket ship ready to blast off—golf balls and all—and a castle created to look like a medieval fortress, complete with knights and ladies and an enormous catapult.

It really seemed, as they walked along, that anything—and everything—was possible in the outlandish world of Riverside Mini-Golf.

Madison only hoped that her adventure would continue *off* the mini-golf course, too—for a long, long time.

Chapter 17

Madison sat and counted shadows on the ceiling, but her eyelids would not close. She had many different things bouncing around inside her brain at the same time.

First there were Dad and Stephanie's arguments.

Then there was the upcoming hatchling night.

And of course there was the flip-flop-flipping crush on Will.

Madison pulled out her best companion: her laptop. Thanks to Dad's help, the laptop was working again.

She clicked open her e-mailbox. Aimee had sent her an e-mail with an attachment. It was a copy of some article that had just appeared in the Far Hills newspaper. Madison opened that file and read it first, with great interest.

THE FAR HILLS GAZETTE

Tuesday, August 17
Far Hills, NY

Weather today: Patchy clouds, humid, high 80s

The Last Ballet by R. J. Westerlybrook

Everyone in the room at 274 Goethe Avenue spoke in hushed tones and watched as Ecatarina Elaine Rudofsky, formerly of Kazakhstan, led the girls in a short routine.

The elderly ballerina standing at the front of the room looked wistful as she bowed and bent from the waist. She twisted her arms up into the air and looked off into the distance, chest heaving with emotion. All girls in the room, themselves dressed in pink-and-white floral prints, wiped away tears.

This month, Far Hills celebrates twenty years of the Madame Elaine Dance Studio. A popular school for young girls at the beginning, middle, and advanced stages of their ballet experience, Madame Elaine's has been a primary destination for ballerinas from all over Far Hills and the surrounding areas.

This year, however, Madame Elaine has decided to close her doors. Sources say a new ballet instructor may take over part of the old business and revamp the facilities to welcome new students. But the elderly ballerina finds that it is time to retire.

"I don't know what we will do without her," said Ranya Roberts, a ballet student of Madame Elaine's for more than two years and a Far Hills middle-schooler.

Madame Elaine, who has more than 112 students in her many groups, has her eye on the future, naming students she believes are certain to have a rich life on and off the stage—no matter what the fate of the studio may be.

"I was only just telling one of my best students, Aimee Gillespie, to practice something a hundred times. Not because I believe that practice makes perfect, but because I believe that the heart of good dance comes from the little moments inside and out, done over and over."

(Continued 2C)

Madison turned back to Aimee's latest blog entry. It had been posted the night before, along with the short newspaper article.

08-17

So u probably read the article about my dance teacher's studio since I e-mailed it to all of u. I cried ALL last nite. ">(Whatamigonnado?

Some of the other students think someone might take over the studio--they should!--but I don't believe it. NO one can take over for Madame Elaine. It's so weird b/c she was hard on me this yr. She was real picky about my dancing and my legwork but now--no one will be as good a teacher as her. Mom thinks they're changing the space into a beauty salon or something! She heard that from Olga, that real estate broker who lives down the st. from us. That can't be true, can it?

What if i have to go to Westlake or some other town to dance? I wish I knew what was REALLY happening. Madame Elaine is having this HUGE party for us all next wk. after the performances. She says we'll all be pleasantly surprised by the plan for the studio. Whatever that means. I'm not pleasantly anything right now. You know it's a bad scene when my brothers are being all nice to me about it. Last nite Roger was here for dinner & he brought me daisies!!! OMG!!! Billy, Dean, and Doug were all letting me watch whatever I wanted on TV. They NEVER do that. Mom and Dad must have told them to be nice to me. I know u guys would be sooooo supportive.

What will i do if I don't have my dance classes???

I hope things are better in the other parts of the universe like CA, FL, and England. Nobody posted in the blog yesterday so everyone better post right now. I could use sum cheering up pleez.

CUL8R . . . xox

p.s.: don't forget that when u all get back u have 2 come over & watch the video of me performing, ok?

Madison didn't hesitate after reading Aimee's e-mail. She got up off her bed, turned on the light, and slipped down the hallway.

Stephanie was sitting in the living room with a book. Dad was near her with his BlackBerry, poking at the buttons. Some kind of classical music was on the stereo—maybe Mozart. Or was it Beethoven? Madison always heard classical tunes playing at Dad's apartment, and she was beginning to be able to tell one composer from another.

"Hey," Madison said softly as she padded over to the sofa.

Stephanie was surprised to see Madison. "I didn't even hear you walk in," she said. "Is everything okay?"

Madison frowned. "Not really. I just checked my e-mail, and I got this note from Aimee, and she is so bummed out, and I just feel so bad. . . ."

"What's the matter with Aimee?" Stephanie asked.

Dad poked his head up. "Is there a problem?" he asked.

"It's the most awful thing, but they're closing Aim's dance studio," Madison said. "Can you believe it? Anyway, I wanted to ask if—I know it's late—but I wanted to maybe call her up on the phone, to check in."

Dad shrugged from across the room. "There's the phone," he said simply, pointing to it. "It's still just before ten o'clock. Stephanie, do you have a problem with that?"

"Well, Aimee is probably asleep," she said. "Won't her parents mind?"

"A call from Maddie?" Dad laughed. "Trust me. Aimee's mom and dad invented the words 'laid back'—*way* back. They won't care if it's a call from Maddie. She's practically part of their family, too."

Madison knew that Mr. and Mrs. Gillespie probably wouldn't even know she was calling, since they hardly ever picked up their phone. They always left the answering of the phone to their kids.

So, with Dad and Stephanie's permission, Madison grabbed the portable and dialed Far Hills. It rang four times before someone picked up.

"Hello," a voice grumbled. It was deep, and Madison could tell whose it was. "Is this Dean?" Madison asked.

"Who is this?" Dean replied.

Madison explained and then asked to speak with Aimee, who was not yet asleep, as Stephanie and Dad had suspected.

Aimee came to the phone right away.

"Hello?" Aimee asked politely. "Who is this?"

"Aim?" Madison said.

"*Maddie!*" Aimee squealed. "Oh, my God, did you get the telepathic signals I was sending you right now? I can't believe this is really you on the telephone. I swear on a stack of Bibles I was just sitting here thinking about you this very minute, right now!"

Madison giggled. Aimee always branded herself a nonbeliever in things like fortune-telling and fate. Madison knew she was just being sarcastic, but she played along with Aimee's rush of enthusiasm.

"I didn't get any psycho—er, psychic—signals," Madison joked. "But I had to call anyway."

"You read my blog," Aimee said matter-of-factly. "Didn't you?"

"I'm sorry, Aim," Madison said sympathetically.

"Isn't it awful?" Aimee said.

"Well, you told me you didn't really like Madame Elaine," Madison said, trying to sound supportive without sounding dismissive.

"I didn't—I don't—" Aimee started to say. Her voice trembled a little bit as she spoke. She sounded as if she were still crying.

"Aim?" Madison asked slowly. "I'm giving you a very big hug right now, so you have to stop crying. Okay?"

There was heavy silence over the phone line.

"I can't stop," Aimee admitted, sobbing more softly now.

Madison hadn't heard Aimee cry like that before, and she felt helpless being so far away.

"Vacation is almost over," Madison said, trying to sound cheery. "Soon we'll all be back at Far Hills in the classroom, and everything will go back to the way it was."

"Except Madame Elaine's," Aimee said.

"I wish I were there," Madison said. "So I could help you feel better."

The silence over the phone line returned. Madison heard music playing softly in the background.

"I'm tired," Aimee admitted. "I should go."

"Okay," Madison said.

"By the way, how's camp?" Aimee asked before hanging up. "I'm sorry I didn't even ask. And you haven't posted a blog in a day or more."

"Camp's cool," Madison said. "I know I need to write in the blog. I will. Promise. When we hang up."

"Go write something now. I'll check in the morning," Aimee said. Madison thought it sounded as though Aimee were smiling.

"Good night, Aim," Madison said.

As they hung up the phones, a dozen questions zipped into Madison's head. How was Blossom (Aimee's dog)? How was her dad's bookstore, where Aimee sometimes worked part-time? And most important: how was Hart Jones? With all the other things on her mind, Madison had almost forgotten about Hart.

Almost.

The truth was that Hart was never very far from her thoughts.

Madison placed the portable phone back in its charger and headed back to her laptop. After all of the night's blog entries, she needed to dash off a quick entry of her own.

When she returned to bigfishbowl.com, however, she found the unread entries from her other two BFFs. First there was a long, funny one from Lindsay.

08-17

This has been the most GROOViESt week of my life EVER. First I get to fly overseas with Dad--and from the things he's saying, there's still a good chance that he and my mom will get back together. I know it's like a tennis match the way they stay and go from each other, but I still want them to work it out. WDIK!?

SO. That's all irrelevant because of the amazing thing that happened yesterday. I am still shaking so let me start at the beginning--and NO laughing even though Maddie totally predicted this one. You guys are always saying that someday my prince would come. So here's the update on all that. Instead of my prince coming to me--I came to my prince.

I MET PRINCE HARRY.

Seriously. Are you sitting down? I met him. In person. He actually SHOOK MY HAND!!!! Or, as the locals would say, "He shook my bloody hand!" LOL. (OF course my hand isn't really bloody with blood but u know that, right? DUH.) So I met Prince Harry and what did I do? Almost fainted. Okay, that's not exactly true but I did feel a little heady and dizzy for a split second. It all started when I went with Dad to see this free music concert in early evening near Hyde Park. I guess there was some charity event or something and we saw the motorcade so we were waiting with the other people. As it turns out we were standing at the EXACT spot where they got out of their limos. So there I was dressed in my fat pants (because I have been eating sooo much I don't fit in my other clothes anymore LOL) and I basically came face to face with PRINCE HARRY. Ok, so there were like ten zillion police there too, so my view of the Prince was partially obscured. But then, as if that wasn't good enough--he came over to greet us. He is very handsome in person. I wish it had been his brother, of course, b/c who doesn't want to see Prince William but Harry will do. LOL. I threw my arm out and up and then wiggled to the front of this barricade that had been set up on the spot. And there I was in the front, hand out-- and his fingers touched my fingers for just a split second but our hands touched--OMG. I wanted to say hello or something--anything. I didn't. I almost shut my eyes, actually. This has to be one of the top five days of my life. EVER.

P.S.: I know u won't believe this but the best day in the galaxy got EVEN BETTER when I came back fm our day. There was an e-mail in my mailbox fm DAN. Can u believe it? I'm afraid 2 read it. It's probably nothing but ... :>)

P.P.S.: I come home tomorrow (Friday) psyched! We all get 2 c each other hooray!!!!!!!!!!!!!!!!!!!!!!

Madison laughed out loud.

The blogs didn't end there. The cursor flashed on Fiona's blog. She'd finally written a new entry, too. And much to Madison's surprise, Fiona had a very different story to tell about Julio—and other topics—that day.

08-17

Only one thing on my mind this morning: I'm ready 2 come home. I love being back here in Los Gatos but I miss my life in Far Hills SOOOO MUCH. Isn't that weird? I always was SUCH a California girl and now--I'm just NOT. You'll be happy 2 know that Dad and Mom told me that they won't be moving back to CA anytime soon, despite previous reports to the contrary. Dad was just feeling nostalgic (he says). I guess they talked about it pretty seriously but decided our new house (in FH) is great and our new schools (in FH) are great and our new life (w/all of U!) is great. We talked at dinner last nite. Even Chet said he didn't want to come back--and he misses his CA skater friends way more than I miss my old friends.

P.S.: I told Maddie a little bit about seeing this old guy friend Julio when I was here. Well, it was just weird and nothing happened. NOTHING. I'll tell u Aim & Lindsay more when I C U. I'll be back home really late on Fri.

Madison sighed. After nearly two weeks apart, the four BFFs had been worried about how they'd survive. But they had survived intact. They'd uncovered new summer stories and revisited old summer stories. They'd met up with old friends and shared things with new friends. They'd found a dozen ways to hit the beach and make things really happen.

And it wasn't even over yet for Madison. She still had hatchling night to look forward to.

Madison hit NEW and typed into her blog, just as she'd promised Aimee she would. Her BFF would check for the new page in just a few short hours— and Madison wanted to be there, waiting.

08-18
I hope we never have 2 be apart again for more than a week at a time. It feels like this past wk was hard 4 everyone--including me. OMG Thanx 4 being so honest about

224

stuff. None of u are alone!!! OK so I have this confession
2 make--I am still crushing on this Will guy so I made a
list of all the things I like about both him & Hart. OK--
ready??

<u>Will</u>
Calls me Mad Dog
Blond hair, messy
No glasses
Trendy clothes
Smart
From NYC

<u>Hart</u>
Calls me Finnster
Brown hair that's messy
Wears glasses sometimes
Nice dresser
Super smart!!
From Far Hills

When I read the list, I can't even tell them apart. Which makes
me more confused than ever. So again I just want u 2 know UR
NOT ALONE (Fiona!!!) and u shouldn't feel bad just because u
made a mistake or liked someone else. I think everything happens
4 a reason, right?

This has been a week of surprises (Prince Harry!
No more dance studio! OMG!!!!!) and I miss u all
more than words. We need 2 be 2gether soon. This
whole week I thought it was all about my crushes and
boys and doing the coolest thing. But now I wonder if
that's what it's all about. What do u think??? What is it
all about?????

OK. I have 2 go now and get ready to watch turtles lay eggs in
the dark and I wonder if maybe THAT is what it's all about. Yours till
the heart breaks . . . or NOT! No, definitely NOT--no heartbreak
here, pleez!!!

p.s.: Thanks 2 everyone for being the VERY BEST BLOGGERHEADS in the whole universe. U made this week go by soooooooo much faster.

LYLAS--FAE! FAE! FAE!!! :>)

Chapter 18

Because hatchling night began with the last moments of sundown and continued into the very late nighttime hours, Thursday's camp session didn't officially begin until seven o'clock in the evening. That gave Madison more time to check blogs and write e-mails. It also gave her time to surf the Internet and look up random information about loggerhead turtles.

She had plenty to keep herself busy, which is exactly what she did.

Madison skimmed some of the last-minute notes she'd scribbled on a notepad. She needed to remember that stuff.

* Loggerheads roamed the oceans by millions, but no longer
* ? can drown in shrimp trawls (what??) and other fishing gear
* ? can die from pollutants or swallowing trash they think is food (plastic on soda 6-pks)
* hatchlings who get disoriented by lights near beach wander away from the ocean and get crushed by cars
* nesting season runs a long time fm May 1–October 31

She took a lot of notes, but of all the facts Madison had learned at Camp Sunshine, what she'd learned most of all was that she still had a lot left to learn! Hatchling night was some kind of symbolic beginning, wasn't it?

Madison was learning to see the world around her in a new way. Not only was she seeing new animals and meeting new people, but she was finding ways to see in the dark. Or at least she hoped so. Madison needed to have good night vision in order to watch the loggerheads digging in the sand under a white, glowing moon.

As the time to head to the ELC grew closer, Madison began to feel butterflies in her stomach. She assumed at first that this was because of Will.

But as time went on, she wondered if it had more to do with someone—or something—else. Maybe all this feeling was just about the turtles, plain and simple.

Could it be that simple?

Dad drove Madison to the ELC as the sun dipped lower in the sky. The air had cooled off some, thankfully. The last week had been hotter than the week before it. But now there was actually a bit of a breeze.

Madison spotted Ann and Suchita standing together near the side of the building. She hustled over to them. "Hey," she said. "It's so weird to be starting camp when it's getting dark, isn't it?"

It was nearly eight o'clock. There was still a lot of light left in the sky, but night was coming, and (Madison hoped) so were the turtles.

"Yes," Suchita said. "My mother didn't want me to come. She's worried."

Ann held up a mini tape-recording device. She planned to record a blow-by-blow account of hatchling night—and maybe write an article on it for her school paper—or even her local newspaper back in Cleveland. Just like Madison, Ann had made a scratch-pad list of notes about loggerheads. Madison admired Ann's motivation.

On the edge of the beach, Leonard and the camp staffers made sure all of the groups were present and accounted for.

"Look up at the sky," Leonard advised. "We have

229

an almost-full moon. We have a sea ahead of us and a sea above us. Just look at that sea of stars, boys and girls. Even though the moon is bright, I can still see the Little Dipper. Can you?"

Madison liked the fact that Leonard was talking all poetically about the sea and stars. It inspired her, and she wondered if maybe she should write a poem of her own about this night, about this entire camp experience. Maybe she could send it to Bigwheels.

Will, Teeny, and Logan were standing off to the side. When Leonard stopped talking for a moment, the boys trudged over to where the girls from the Egrets stood. Madison could sense Will's approach; even though it was dark and she couldn't see well, Madison was fairly sure he had a determined look in his eyes.

"Maddie!" Will called out before he'd even gotten to her.

Madison stepped aside so Ann was the first person Will ran into—literally. As luck would have it, Will tripped on the sand near the edge of the berm and nearly plowed into Ann.

Suchita laughed. Logan came over, also laughing. Meanwhile, Ann reached out and helped Will get up from the sand.

Madison took a deep breath of the sea air. It smelled like salt and dampness, and she wished she could go for a swim. The moon was hitting the water beautifully. She scanned the sand for some sign of turtle life, but there was nothing yet.

"Maddie, where are your night goggles?" Teeny asked.

Madison laughed. "I left them at home," she said.

Just then, Leonard approached the cluster of Egrets.

"I will be making announcements on the beach during hatchling night," Leonard said. "Does everyone have insect repellent on?"

He had a walkie-talkie in his hand, as did most of the counselors, to be able to communicate across the span of beach.

Leonard's voice echoed in the night air. "I just wanted to remind all of you that there is no flash photography and there are no flashlights allowed. Lights disrupt the nesting turtles and can disorient them. Okay?"

Madison nodded. All the talk about the turtles had her really excited, and although she'd just reviewed her notes, she had nearly forgotten the importance of keeping the baby and mother turtles out of the light.

From where they stood on the side of the beach, Madison and the rest of the Egrets could see the area where some of the nests had already been built, where the hatchlings were expected to hit the beach. The night was very still. Everyone kept their eyes on the sand. If all went as planned, the silver moon would provide all the light needed for a pathway from ocean to sand. Once the first turtles climbed out of the sea, the campers would move on to the beach for full observation.

Ann steadied her tape recorder as she whispered into it. "Waiting for the turtles," she said.

Patiently, everyone waited for a change in the horizon, a break in the surface of the water. The buzz of Leonard's walkie-talkie and the others was a foreign sound compared to the easy gush of waves breaking onshore—and the low, consistent chirp of crickets. The tide was rising.

Madison heard Leonard's voice cut across the night air.

"Loggerheads. Due north."

The campers spun around. Then, led by counselors holding little red lights (because red light was not off limits), they moved toward the north. Everyone wanted a look at a turtle as it made its move on to the beach.

But the group got more than it bargained for. As one turtle slowly dragged its body up on to the sand, the cluster of campers hung back, waiting and watching. Then, all at once, at least a dozen more turtles appeared at the waterline, and, just like that, the beach seemed covered with turtles. More specifically, turtles on a mission.

The moonlight was the best light for watching

the turtles. It was enough for observation yet it let the campers remain relatively undetected. Of course, with that many campers on the sand, it was tricky to keep a low profile. The group worked very hard to do so.

Madison, Ann, and Suchita ended up together again. They followed one very large female logger-head to an area of sand closer up near the dunes and watched as she began to dig her nest. Sand flew as she dug deeper still. By the time she began dropping her eggs, the three camp friends were ready to burst into applause.

Leonard came over to watch, with the girls. He asked Madison and the others to form a semicircle so he could help identify the turtle's age. "See all those barnacles on her shell?" he asked.

Madison nodded.

"She's a mature loggerhead, this girl," Leonard said. He was smiling. "I feel like I should know her. She's been around the sea a few times."

Leonard pressed closer as the turtle continued to lay her eggs. He had one of the staffers come over with a little red light and shine it on to the egg drop. Madison was in awe of the entire process. The eggs sat neatly in the sand as the turtle added more and more to the pile.

When it seemed as though the turtle had com-pleted her egg-laying, Madison and the others beat a steady retreat south. They needed to give the loggerhead the space she needed to make her way back to the ocean.

No sooner had the turtle gone than Will reappeared.

"Did you just watch her lay eggs?" Will asked breathlessly. Logan and Teeny were with him.

Madison, Ann, and Suchita described the events as they had just happened. Unfortunately, the boys had not yet witnessed an egg-laying. Will looked sorely disappointed.

A buzz from another walkie-talkie, however, sent the boys off in another direction. There were more loggerheads coming on to the beach, in different shapes and sizes.

"This is one of the most amazing nights of my life," Suchita said, speaking the words that both Madison and Ann were also feeling.

Ann seconded the remark. "I feel like these past two weeks are nothing compared to this right now. Wow," she said.

"I like that we're doing this with just the three of us," Madison said. "It reminds me of how I do stuff with my BFFs back home."

Ann checked her watch. "I can't believe it's already ten o'clock. I wonder how much longer we'll be here."

Leonard walked around the beach with his red light, searching for signs of life in the sand. He pointed out different sets of tracks. It seemed as though all the information that the campers had learned for the past ten days or so was being put to good use.

Madison stood on the sand next to the two friends she had never expected to have and felt very thankful. Although she still missed her BFFs more than anything, this night nearly made up for all the pangs of loneliness she'd felt.

"I can't believe it's over now," Ann said dejectedly, as if she'd only just realized that fact.

"It went by so fast," Suchita said.

"Maybe we can stay in touch," Madison suggested. "We could be keypals. Or e-pals or something."

"What's a keypal?" Ann asked.

Madison explained. She told both girls about her long-distance relationship with Vicki, aka Bigwheels. She also mentioned bigfishbowl.com. Much to Madison's surprise, neither girl had ever heard of it before.

By then the activity on the beach had subsided a little. No one seemed tired, even though it was getting close to eleven o'clock. Suchita wandered off to talk to someone from the Alligators group; that left Madison on her own with Ann.

"So, you were right after all," Madison said. "I guess we were meant to be friends."

Ann shrugged. "But I'm so bummed out."

"Why?" Madison asked.

Ann looked as though she wanted to cry. "I don't know," she said, sniffling. "It's just that—I don't have—well, I told you my friend Patti sort of blew me off, and I don't have that many friends, and—now you're going home—"

Madison put her arm lightly around Ann's shoulder. "Don't worry," she said gently. "What about the turtles? What about tonight? What about Will? You still like him, right?"

Ann looked squarely at Madison. "I'm not stupid. I know he doesn't like me. Not like that. No one does."

Madison didn't know what to say. It was as if Ann had suddenly become this whole other person—as if the real (genuine, honest, not-full-of-herself) Ann had been holed up inside all week. Now she came pouring out.

"I'm sorry for being such a downer," Ann said. "See? Now I probably ruined tonight for you. Figures."

Madison shook her head. "No way," she said. "No one could ruin tonight. It was as close to perfect as it gets. Doncha think?"

Ann sniffled again. Then she smiled. "I guess so. Yeah, you're right. It was pretty perfect."

"We can stay in touch," Madison said.

"I know," Ann said. "Wow, I'm so embarrassed that I got emotional. I can't believe—"

"Surprise!"

236

From nowhere (well, from somewhere on the dark, dark beach), Teeny popped out and scared Madison and Ann.

"Gotcha!" he cried, even louder.

Someone a few feet away said "*Shhhhhh!*" so that Teeny wouldn't disturb one of the last turtles still nesting on the beach.

"That was the most awesome thing I have ever, *ever* seen," Teeny went on, ignoring the staff member who had shushed him. "And I live in Florida!"

At that moment, Will and Logan came up to join the conversation.

"What's up?" Logan asked the girls and Teeny.

"You guys finally saw a turtle lay her eggs?" Madison asked.

Will nodded. "It was as cool as you said."

Madison looked at Will and then over at Ann. For some reason, in that moment, in the middle of the beach, in the middle of the night under a pale moon, things seemed to make sense. In that moment, Madison realized that she didn't really have the crush on Will that she thought she had. What she realized was that someone else had a crush that was much bigger than hers.

Here, in the half-darkness, these fast friends had shared the experience of a lifetime. Madison wanted to make sure, for Ann's sake, that the best part of her memory about that night included spending time standing with the cute boy she'd been crushing on all week. Why not? As carefully and subtly as she could, Madison maneuvered herself to the side. She cracked a few more jokes with Teeny and Logan, and the three of them headed back toward the edge of the beach. Will was left standing next to Ann— alone. They had no choice now but to speak to each other under the stars.

And so they did. Or at least Madison hoped they did. She didn't turn around to double-check. She'd find out from Ann in the morning.

Back at the main entrance to the ELC, the parents had parked all along the road and waited to pick up their kids. Madison spotted Dad and Stephanie's car right away. She raced over. Dad was in the driver's seat, with the air conditioner running, the radio tuned to a classical station. The car felt and sounded like a symphony when Madison climbed into the front.

"Hey," Dad said. "So? How was it?"

"No words, Dad," Madison said.

"No words? What's that supposed to mean?"

"Perfection," Madison said. "I can't believe I was that close to a loggerhead turtle, Dad. *This* close! Wow."

Dad's hands were fixed firmly on the steering wheel. He looked very serious.

"Dad? Are you all right?" Madison asked when she noticed his expression.

Dad shook his head. "I've been thinking a lot

tonight, Maddie," he said. "I've been unfair to you these past two weeks. Unfair to you and to Stephanie. I wanted to apologize for that."

Madison felt a heaviness lift from the air around them. This was something that had needed to be said since she'd arrived in Florida.

"I didn't want to get in the way," Madison said. "I mean, between you and Stephanie, that is."

"You aren't in the way," Dad said.

"Well, I know. But remember when you and Mom split up and I asked all those questions and I . . . well, I got in the way."

"No, you didn't!" Dad insisted. "You thought that?"

"Of course," Madison said. "What else was I supposed to think?"

Dad shook his head again as he stopped at a red light. They were close to the apartment building. No one said anything for a moment. Then Dad pulled into the parking garage and turned off the car. They sat in the dark for a minute. Of course, this didn't bother Madison one bit, since she'd been in semi-darkness all night.

"Maddie, I am so sorry," Dad said again.

Dad's spontaneous apology gave Madison courage to ask a question that had been on her mind throughout the entire visit—and throughout all the arguments she had heard between Dad and Stephanie.

"Dad, are you and Stephanie going to get divorced, too?"

Dad's eyes widened when Madison asked that one.

"What made you think *that*?" Dad asked her.

"Well, you hardly speak, and you yell a lot about things that seem so . . . well, serious. Stephanie didn't want to tell me what it was about. She told me I should talk to you."

"Did she?" Dad asked, seemingly pleased.

"So?" Madison asked. "Are you?"

"Definitely not," Dad replied. "Not even close. And the reason Stephanie wanted me to tell you about our arguments was because we have been discussing some serious things."

"If you're not getting divorced, what is it?"

Dad shrugged. "Well . . ."

"Oh, my God!" Madison screeched. "Are you guys having a baby?"

Dad grinned. "Not yet. We've talked about it. But, no, that's not why things have been tense. You see, Stephanie told you she lost her job. And that made us rethink my job, too. . . ."

"Yeah . . ." Madison said, thinking hard.

"Well, we've been talking very seriously about moving."

Madison's head began to whirl. "Moving?" she cried, clutching the side of her seat. She hadn't once thought of that possibility—not ever. In her mind, Dad always lived close by—and had to live close by. But this could change all of that.

"You can't move," Madison quickly said.

Dad calmly took Madison's hand in his own. "We're not going anywhere right now," Dad reassured her. "You would be the very first to know. I promise."

"You can't move," Madison repeated. "You can't. You can't."

She couldn't even wrap her mind around the *idea* of Dad being anywhere other than Far Hills.

"It's very late," Dad said. The green digital clock on the dashboard said it was 12:23 A.M. "You have to be up and out in the morning. Why don't we talk about this some more when you've had a little sleep?"

"Okay," Madison sighed. She was tired, after all. "But you can't move, Dad."

She had to say it one more time, as if that would be the thing that made all the difference. Once inside, despite being super tired, Madison called upon her last reserves of energy. She had to type things in to her laptop files before she forgot them all in the deep, sea air–induced sleep that was certain to come.

The Loggerheads

Rude Awakening: Where there's a Will, there's a way--a way to get him to spend more time with Ann!

I was standing there in the middle of

241

the sand when it dawned on me (kaboom!)
just how much Ann likes this guy--way more
than I ever did (or do). I realized that I
like things the way they are--as far as
Hart goes, that is. I mean, I loved
flirting with Will but I can't take it too
seriously. And Ann likes Will so much more
than I do. Even though there are only two
days left, it's worth a try. Maybe this is
all just me feeling guilty, but it does
feel like the right way to handle all
this. I don't know if Ann and Will belong
together. But I know Madison and Will
don't. My heart (Hart!) is so taken
already. LOL.

Sometimes I feel like I spend all this
time thinking about boys or how other
people think of me--or even worrying too
much about Dad and Stephanie's life. And I
should just STOP. Somehow these wks @ camp
made me see some stuff I'd been missing.
And now I'm pretty sure I know how to fill
in those missing parts. At least, once I
get back to Far Hills, I will know how to
do it right.

Rude Awakening: The loggerheads weren't
the only ones to come out of their shells
last night.

I did, too.

242

Chapter 19

After typing in her laptop until after 1:40 A.M. on Thursday night, Madison could barely drag herself out of bed on Friday morning. However, she got up in time to eat breakfast and dress for camp. There was no way Madison wanted to miss even the teeniest piece of her very last day—no matter how tired she felt.

Dad was off to work before Madison was ready to go, so Stephanie drove Madison over to Camp Sunshine.

"I heard you up very late in your room," Stephanie said. "On your laptop?"

Madison grinned. "Of course."

"I know you and your dad had a nice talk on the way home last night," Stephanie said. "And I'm so glad."

Madison nodded. "Yeah," she said. "I can't believe you're thinking about moving away from Far Hills."

"I know. It's a very serious decision. What with losing my job and the talk of moving, that explains some of the reason I've been so emotional. I'm sorry for that, Maddie. I hope it didn't ruin your time at Camp Sunshine."

"You didn't ruin anything," Madison said. "I was thinking that maybe you and Dad were going to break up."

"Oh," Stephanie said. "No wonder you were concerned."

"Yeah," Madison said, yawning. "You know me. I always overthink this stuff, right?"

"Right," Stephanie said with a smile. "So what's the plan for your final day at camp?"

"Some kind of big luncheon and awards ceremony, I heard," Madison said. "Not that I'll be getting an award for anything."

Stephanie pulled up in front. She leaned across the front seat and kissed Madison on the top of the head—it was a strong, heartfelt kiss.

Inside the doors of the ELC, Leonard and his team had decorated the place from floor to ceiling with everything from artwork the campers had created the week before to green balloons shaped like turtles. Along one wall was a long table set with food for breakfast.

"Maddie!"

244

Ann rushed right over to greet Madison as she walked in. They went to one of the big tables and sat down together. As they were sitting there, Madison spotted someone else familiar walking through the front doors. It was Myrtle Shelly—back for a repeat lecture? Madison guessed she had returned to see how hatchling night had gone—and to say her own good-byes.

As it turned out, Myrtle was there to help present awards.

Leonard started up the awards ceremony once everyone in the room had taken a seat. Each of the specific teams got a special mention. Then he started to give out ribbons and certificates to each camper—starting in alphabetical order. Standing up at the podium, Myrtle helped Leonard read off the individual names.

Madison beamed when her name was called. Myrtle handed Madison her certificate, emblazoned with the Camp Sunshine logo and an outline of a large loggerhead turtle on the top.

"Congratulations, my dear," Myrtle said. "I know my husband, Walter, would be very pleased to know you completed your camp days with flair."

Madison smiled and returned to her seat. She felt prouder than proud. Somehow, even though this was a day concerned with ending, it felt like a kind of new beginning.

After the ceremony there was a relaxed party in

which people drifted outdoors and came back. As would be expected, most of the campers stayed within the groups they'd worked with during the two-week stay. The Egrets hung out by the large bay window at the back of the room that overlooked the mangrove swamp.

"So this is good-bye," Teeny said. "Isn't that a huge drag? I actually like you guys," he added.

"Too bad," Will cracked. "Because we don't like you."

Ann laughed out loud—too loud. Madison knew she was just showing off for Will. But it was really no biggie. No one wanted to say or do anything negative today. They talked about all the activities they had shared together—working closely as a group; the scavenger hunt; the bird-watching from the pontoon boat; and watching the turtle-nesting, among other things.

Since it was the final day of camp, things ended way earlier than usual. The parents had been asked to come back to pick everyone up at two o'clock sharp. By one-thirty, everyone was starting to get all sentimental. Madison asked Anna and Suchita if they wanted to stay connected via e-mail, and both said yes. Madison collected their e-mail addresses. She'd store them in her laptop when she got back to Dad's place.

Will pulled Madison aside at one point during the round of camp good-byes.

"So, this is over, huh?" he said.

Madison nodded. "Yeah. It was fun. Your grandpa Ralph is a nice guy."

"Yeah, mini-golf was mad fun," Will said. "Will you be back next summer?"

"I don't know. Probably not," Madison said. "My mom's a film producer. I think I want to go on a vacation with her."

"Whoa," Will said. "Your mom makes movies? I forgot you told me that."

"Well, documentaries."

"So . . . I guess I won't see you again, then?" he asked, sounding a little dejected.

"I guess not," Madison said, covering up the disappointment in her own voice. She'd been so sure last night about Will and Ann, but now, standing next to Will, the familiar crush feelings returned.

"Unless—" Will said, "unless maybe we see each other sometime in New York. I mean, we practically are neighbors, right?"

"Right," Madison said. "So, you should E me sometime."

"Yeah, totally," Will said. He sounded happy about that. "Bye."

"Bye," Madison said. She turned and walked away. After a moment, she realized that she hadn't given Will her e-mail address. She almost turned around to write it down for him, but then she stopped herself. Maybe it was better not to. She remembered the time she'd met that boy Mark at Gramma Helen's house. She'd wanted to e-mail him, too, after they'd spent time together at the lake. But it never happened.

Things like that never happened.

Madison kept moving toward the exit. She said her good-byes to Leonard and the other members of the camp staff. Then she stopped off at a large table set up by the door. She needed to pick up her official Camp Sunshine T-shirt and visor.

The room was overflowing with kids and their parents. Madison searched for Suchita and Logan to say good-bye, but couldn't find them anywhere. Then she looked for Teeny. He gave her a big wave from across the room. After that, Madison sneaked out to the parking lot.

After Stephanie took her back to the apartment, Madison packed up as much of her stuff as she could. The flight was leaving the next day at noon. Madison crashed down on her bed, closing her eyes for a few minutes. Or at least, she thought it was only a few minutes.

When she woke up, however, it was nearly din-nertime.

"So, I guess you were exhausted," Dad said when they sat down to eat. "It's been quite a week, hasn't it?"

"I second that one," Stephanie said knowingly.

Dad reached for Stephanie's hand across the table. He kissed it.

"Quite a week," he repeated. Then he grabbed Madison's hand, too—and squeezed it.

Madison couldn't believe how tired she actually was. It was from the previous night—and all the nights before that, too. Despite any sentimental feelings earlier in the day or even right now, Madison was ready to get back to Far Hills. She missed her pillows—and of course she missed her best pillow of all, Phinnie. She'd spoken to Mom that morning. Phinnie had, as usual, been sleeping on Madison's bed every night since she'd been away.

After dinner, Madison washed up, finished packing, and logged on to bigfishbowl.com. She hadn't checked her e-mailbox in a while.

And there was important mail.

Very important mail.

FROM	SUBJECT
✉ Sk8ingboy	Sorry no E-MAIL
✉ GoGramma	Photos, please!
✉ TheEggMan	F.W.
✉ Bigwheels	My bro & other stuff

Madison clicked on the first e-mail on the list. After two weeks of not getting one single note from Hart, there it was.

It was short, but very, very sweet. The strange thing about Hart's e-mail was the fact that he'd written it a few days earlier. Somehow it had gotten stuck in the server—and had not been delivered until today.

But it had arrived, nonetheless, and Madison had to smile as she read it once, twice, and then a third time—before hitting SAVE.

From: Sk8ingboy
To: MadFinn
Subject: Sorry no E-MAIL
Date: Wed 18 Aug 7:51 PM
So I know u won't believe me but I
swear I wrote a couple of times.
It keeps coming back 2 me. Stupid
e-mail account I have 2 switch. I
don't know why my e-mail is so
messed.

Things here are ok. Boring as
usual. The other day at the pool a
little girl went under the water
and I guess u could say I saved
her. So that was a big deal for me.
I went to the movies with Egg,
Drew, and Dan the other night and
that was good. Have u talked 2
anyone?

How is camp? I heard from Aim that
u are having fun. I hope so. I
can't wait until you come back. Bye
for now. Send me a postcard or
something. LOL.

Hart

Then Madison opened Gramma Helen's e-mail.
She'd heard from Mom about the great times at
Camp Sunshine—and wanted Madison to forward
her some photos of the setting—and of her new
friends. Madison hit SAVE. She could write a letter
back to Gramma when she was on the plane going
home.

She went on to Egg's e-mail. Madison knew
he'd been e-mailing Fiona for a week with no reply
from her, so Madison hit FORWARD and sent a copy on
to Fiona. She imagined her BFF all the way in Los
Gatos, California, dealing with the whole Julio
thing—and then getting some crazy Egg-mail.
Madison was surprised that Fiona and Egg's relationship had taken a different turn over the vacation—
and curious to see how it would all wind up between
them.

The e-mail Madison truly had been waiting for—
maybe even more than she'd been waiting for
Hart's—was the one from Bigwheels.

Madison read it quickly.

From: Bigwheels
To: MadFinn
Subject: Camp & other stuff
Date: Fri 20 Aug 6:27 PM

So I haven't written in a short
time b/c camp has been SUPER BUSY.
We have these long horseback rides
and then chores and cooking to do @
the ranch so sometimes I have like
NO time to write letters 2 people
like U!

These are just a few of the things
I've done since I've been here:

 · Horseback riding (Western)
 · Sailing
 · Arts & Crafts
 · Nature Trail Hunts
 · Archery
 · Creative Skits
   (like acting & improv)

The camp where I'm at is called
Circle8--Infinity Dude Ranch and
they have 70 different horses. I
ride a dif. one every day if I
want although I love this one
horse called Spaz. Isn't that
the best name for a horse--or for
anything? :>)

The only bad thing is that it's raining too much and I miss my family. My brother is actually here @ the same camp b/c they have people who work w/autistic kids. He is having a blast too.

Write back soon ok?

Yours till the dude ranches,

Vicki aka Bigwheels

After reading it through a second time, Madison hit REPLY.

From: MadFinn
To: Bigwheels
Subject: Re: Camp & other stuff
Date: Fri 20 Aug 8:04 PM

Thanks for your great letter, as usual giving me the best advice and all that--from so far away. Yr camp sounds WICKED--as in amazing/ incredible/BIG WOW. I wish I could ride horses like you. Tell me more in yr next e-mail ok???

This has been a nutty summer in a way b/c I've spent a lot of time alone. N e way, thanks and I just

wanted to send you this attachment
(that I cut & pasted here 2)--it's
a poem I wrote last nite about the
whole turtle camp. I thought u'd
like it since u write poems. U
still write poems, right? Send me
one soon. I think I might actually
save this and turn it in for
English class. I know my teacher
Mr. Gibbons would like it.

Yours till the root beer floats
(b/c I have the biggest craving for
one of those right now!)

Maddie

No Title Yet

She's on belly digging, flippers
Like feet and arms and she's half in and
Half out of the pit and then
She comes and goes back
To the sea (like me)
Meanwhile I see babies hatched
into sand crawling
To the water's edge
Like they're late to meet
Someone there
Everyone's looking for someone
Down below sand you'll find eggs

Up above sky you'll see stars
And someone waiting (like me)
for the turtles to come home

((attachment : TURTLEPOEM.pdf))

P.S.: this poem has no title yet I
might call it LIKE ME but I'm not
sure. Is it like me? What am I like
these days?

P.P.S.: Maybe I should just call it
TURTLES? Oh I don't know anything
anymore :) LYLAS!!!

Chapter 20

The warm sunlight poured into Madison's bedroom and she lay there, under the down comforter, smiling. At first she'd been so unsure about coming to Florida to visit with Dad and Stephanie. Leaving her BFFs seemed the worst of it.

And it had been hard to be without them—or Phin—or Mom for that matter, for two long weeks.

But somehow the kids at Camp Sunshine had made the trip to Florida worthwhile. And it wasn't just the other kids. It was the loggerhead turtles, the pelicans, and even the lizards that scampered across the grounds of the ELC.

Madison dragged herself out of bed once and for all and tried to finish up the bit of packing she had left. From the pocket of her orange bag, she retrieved the very special turtle charms that she had purchased earlier in the trip. Madison held them in her palm. They would be beautiful reminders of the magic that had happened on the beach the night before.

She dragged her suitcase, which was on wheels, into the dining room of the apartment and grabbed a granola bar. Then she picked up a pad of blank paper, sat down, wrote a note, and shoved it into her pocket. She grabbed a skinny bottle with a twist-off lid from the recycling bin, and shoved *that* into her pocket, too.

Madison was nearly halfway out the door before she said, "I'm going for one last walk before we go to the airport, okay?"

"Have a nice time, Maddie," Dad said. He promised to watch—and wave to—Madison from his newspaper-reading perch on their terrace.

Madison tiptoed around the palm fronds that had fallen from the trees onto the back lawn of Dad's apartment complex. Slowly she made her way to a long path that ran parallel to the beachfront. Then she cut across that path and walked down to the beach.

The sand was cool this morning. Madison smiled at the thought that there might be little turtle eggs everywhere under the sand. She saw the whole beach differently now than she had at first.

The tide had pulled out pretty far. Low tide was a beautiful sight. She loved the way the packed sand looked with just a thin layer of water on it. Moving closer, she danced her toes in that water. She'd miss this beach—a lot.

Madison had smuggled along one of Dad and Stephanie's recycled water bottles. She also had written a note: TO WHOM IT MAY CONCERN.

To Whom It May Concern:
    I believe in the power of the ocean. You must, too, since you're reading this. Where did this wash up on shore?
    I believe in turtles that come back to nest after two years and know exactly where to go. I believe in the power of friendship. I hope this note gets somewhere all the way across the Atlantic. And I hope you believe in something, too.
    Write me a note back and tell me what it is. Good—bye 4 now!
                Madison Francesca Finn
                Far Hills, New York
P.S.: go to www.bigfishbowl.com
2 find me! :>)

Madison carefully rolled up the note and stuffed

it into the water bottle. She'd thought about writing something more personal or more fun, but changed her mind at the last minute. This note would do just fine. There was only one chance in a zillion that someone would find it and write back anyway, right? She'd included the Web site at the end just in case that one-in-a-zillion thing occurred.

The water was peaceful-looking—and sounding—as it lapped at the shore. Madison zoned out staring at the waves. She wanted to remember that place—that moment—that ocean—just like *that*.

Before heading back to Dad's apartment, Madison plucked three pink-and-perfect shells off the beach. She would hand-deliver one to each of her BFFs as soon as she was back home.

Good-byes at the West Palm Beach airport a few hours later didn't take long. Dad and Stephanie gave Madison big hugs and thanked her for coming to Florida. Madison, of course, thanked them for treating her to two of the most interesting (and challenging) weeks that she'd ever had.

And then Madison Finn boarded the plane, with laptop in hand. Throughout the ride she found herself daydreaming about the turtles on the beach. Madison looked out the plane window; instead of clouds she saw foam, like ocean foam. She saw the sea in everything.

By the time she landed back in New York City,

Madison had composed a new version of the poem she had sent to Bigwheels. Madison would have to send it later that night. She liked the way seeing the turtles had inspired her to write more. Keeping the blog had inspired her to do the same.

Madison had to wait on the plane until nearly everyone disembarked. She was following the thirteen-and-under rule; the same one she had followed on the flight down. Once all the other passengers had gotten off, Madison found her way to the exit door. She grabbed her orange bag and walked into the main terminal.

Many of the people from Madison's flight had disappeared into the restrooms, down to the baggage-claim area, and over to ground transportation. Madison walked along with one of the flight attendants, searching for some sign of Mom. She was ready to end the trip with a warm hug.

But then something unexpected happened. She saw Mom standing there, but not alone. Standing next to Mom were Fiona, Aimee, and Lindsay. They held up a piece of poster board with words written on it.

WELCOME HOME!!!
MADDIE WE LUV U

Madison wanted to burst into happy tears, but she didn't. Instead, she ran all the way to them and threw open her arms.

"Maddie!" Aimee shrieked, dancing up and down on her toes, as she often did.

Fiona's braids were piled high on her head and she had on a new T-shirt that read CALI GRRL. She threw her arms into the air as if to say, *You're back! At last!*

Lindsay looked the most changed, almost as if she'd had a fashion makeover. She wore funky leather sandals and a peasant blouse, with ripped jeans. And she'd actually gotten a little tanned, which seemed odd, since it had happened on her trip to England, a place not particularly known for its tanning.

Madison sighed a really good sigh. Seeing all three of her friends standing there like that made her head hum. They all looked so . . . *huggable*. Here they'd all four of them gone off to different corners of the world, yet here they were, back again, together again. Next to seeing the turtles laying eggs in the moonlight, this was the most satisfying feeling Madison could remember having had in a long time.

After retrieving Madison's suitcase, they walked back to Mom's car arm in arm. There was another surprise waiting there: Phinnie. Mom had left him in the car with a dish of water and the window rolled down.

And that wasn't the last surprise of the afternoon. Not by a long shot.

They got into the car and started the drive back

toward home, but somewhere in Far Hills, Mom made a sharp left turn where she usually made a right. So, instead of going toward Blueberry Street, Mom drove over to the Far Hills pool.

"Are you kidding?" Madison said when she realized where they were going. "We're going to the pool? Now?"

"Of course!" Aimee snickered. "Someone is waiting for you!"

Fiona smiled. "He was over at our house last night with Chet, and he said your name, like, ten times, Maddie, I swear. *Ten times*."

Lindsay just smiled. "You are so lucky," she said.

"I'm lucky?" Madison joked. "You're the one who got to meet Prince Harry!"

Everyone chuckled. Even Phin wagged his tail.

Madison nuzzled her pug's head. "I missed you so much," she whispered in his ear. Naturally, Phin barked once in response. That meant "Me, too!"

"So what happened to that guy Will?" Fiona said with a grin.

Madison shot her a look back.

Mom pricked up her ears. "What guy Will?" she asked.

Madison rolled her eyes. "No one, Mom. Nothing." She didn't feel like explaining. Especially not five minutes before she was supposed to see *him*. Mentioning Will right now was like inviting bad karma onto her reunion with Hart.

Mom let it drop, although Madison was pretty sure she wouldn't let it be forgotten. Sometime that night Madison would get that same question again, only Mom would want a real answer.

"By the way, Maddie, I found out that the dance studio is staying," Aimee said.

Madison smiled. "That's great news."

"Oh, I almost forgot! I got you guys something in Cali," Fiona said. "I left it at home, though. It's a CD from one of my old friend's bands. Isn't that cool? Their band is called Three-Legged Dog, and they rock out."

Madison laughed. "That's a great name."

Lindsay laughed, too. "Wait until you guys see what I got you in London," she said. "Well, it's what Dad got, actually. I got the same T-shirt for all of us, and it has the London Underground map on it. It looks really mod."

"Wow," Madison said. "I got you guys something, but they're just shells." She pulled the shells out of a pocket in her bag. "You think shells are lame? I didn't get anyone else *anything*," she said. "So there."

Even Mom laughed at that one. She pulled in to the parking lot at the Far Hills pool. The lot looked filled to capacity.

"Do I look okay?" Madison asked her friends.

Everyone nodded at the same time. They were more eager for her to go see Hart than she was.

They jumped out of the car and walked four abreast, like superheroes, as they entered the pool area. Madison didn't know it, but her friends had actually made plans for *everyone* to meet up there. So when they walked inside, Madison saw Egg, Drew, Dan, and Chet. Then she saw Hart, sitting up on one of the lifeguard seats. He was blowing his whistle.

And he looked cuter than cute. Madison's heart thumped. She felt as though they were all watching her, which of course they were. It was like being on reality TV, only weirder.

"Hey, Finnster!" Hart yelled from his seat. He got someone to take over for him and came over. He would have run if running had been allowed, Madison guessed, but Hart was a stickler for pool rules.

Everyone hung around as Madison said her hellos to all the guys. She noticed that Lindsay and Dan were standing close together, while Fiona and Egg were not. Madison didn't want to overthink it, but she wondered if something were going on there.

"Did you ever get any of my e-mails?" Hart asked.

Madison shrugged. "I just got one. Today. Something is really messed up with your account, I think."

"Yeah," Hart said.

Aimee stepped in and managed to distract everyone; they all ran over to the side of the pool to say hello to another one of the guys from school.

That left Hart and Madison alone—just for a minute. But it was time enough to say a real hello.

"So, hey . . ." Hart said a little awkwardly.

Madison stared at the whistle around his neck. He had on red lifeguard shorts. He was definitely tanned—*super* tanned.

"I got you something in Florida," Madison said.

"You did?" Hart said.

"Yeah," Madison said. She reached into the side pocket of her orange bag and pulled out the little turtle charm she'd purchased for him.

Hart took it in his hand and closed his fingers in a fist.

"I saw a whole bunch of turtles on the beach, laying eggs, like magic," Madison said. "So I got the charm to catch some of the magic. Does that make any sense?"

"Wow, thanks," he said. "That's cool."

"I have the same one, you know," Madison said.

"The same turtle charm?"

Madison nodded.

Hart smiled. He reached out, took Madison's hand with the hand that wasn't holding the charm, and swung her arm up and back, pulling her closer to him.

Madison remembered the clouds she had seen outside the plane window. All at once, she felt as though she were up there in the sky again, riding on one of those fluffy clouds.

When Aimee, Lindsay, Fiona, and the rest of the guys walked back over a moment later, Hart was *still* holding Madison's hand.

He wasn't afraid to hold it—right there in front of everyone.

For once, Madison wasn't afraid, either.

In fact, she never wanted to let go.

Mad Chat Words:

W^?	What's up?
Nvr say nvr	Never say never
WDYM	What do you mean?
O&O	Over and out
OCN	Of course not
{:>$	I'm very confused
Megaguilt	I feel guiltier than guilty
; >Q	Sniffling; ready to cry
TOTO	Totally, *totally*
Yawn	Putting me to sleep
Brrrrrr	I'm SO cool
MYSM	Miss you so much
IDW2T@I	I don't want to talk about it
RUKM?	Are you kidding me?
WDIK?	What do I know?
FAE	Forever and ever
BFN	Bye for now
FI	Forget it
LMK	Let me know
LYLAS	Love ya like a sista

Madison's Computer Tip

The Internet can be a real lifeline when you're away from home. E-mails, Insta-Messages, and Blogs are all great ways to post thoughts and share ideas. **But sometimes there are thoughts and feelings that aren't meant for public bulletin boards.** I want to make sure that all the things I post online are okay to be seen by *anybody*. Fiona couldn't post anything about that guy Julio, because she wasn't sure who might be reading her blog. Egg could have read it—and that would have been a *major* disaster. I think blogs are good for funny anecdotes and rambling thoughts. Insta-Messages are good for quick, immediate contact, and e-mails are good for more personal messages. Make sure you're careful not only about *whom* you send or post information to online—but about *how* you send or post it.

For a complete Mad Chat dictionary and more about Madison Finn, visit Madison at www.lauradower.com